FEATHER MEDICINE

MEDICINE

Walking in Shoshone Dreamtime: A Family System Constellation

by

Francesca Mason Boring

Llumina Press

This book is a work of fiction. The characters in this book are not intended to accurately represent any specific persons, either living or dead. No events are meant to be actual historical representations. Any similarities to anyone in my family, or yours, are simply the result of our common, multigenerational humanity. The names of Bert Hellinger, Hunter Beaumont, and Rupert Sheldrake are names of actual men who are referenced out of respect for their vision.

Requests for permission to make copies of any part of this work should be mailed to Permissions Department, Llumina Press, PO BOX 772246, CORAL SPRINGS, FL 33077-2246

ISBN: 1-932560-99-8
Printed in the United States of America by Llumina Press

Library of Congress Cataloging-in-Publication Data

Boring, Francesca Mason.
 Feather medicine : walking in Shoshone dreamtime : a family system constellation / by Francesca Mason Boring.
   p. cm.
 ISBN 1-932560-99-8 (pbk. : alk. paper)
 1. Shoshoni Indians--Fiction. I. Title.
 PS3602.O75F43 2004
 813'.6--dc22

                                                    2003027677

DEDICATION

This book is dedicated to those I have loved who have walked in this world, the next world, and the worlds in between. This book is for all the women in my family, both on this side and the other. This book is for Anna, Naomi, Regina, Katrina, Laura, Mildred, Beverly, Ilaine, and of all my nieces and cousins.

I would like to express appreciation to Radley Davis, Pit River, and his willingness to share insight, which contributed to the "Acorn Story". Thank you to Hunter Beaumont for encouraging me to believe that I could tell this story.

I thank my teachers: Lavaun Palla, Larry Gotelli, Beverly LeBeau, Vivien Hailstone and Inez Larson, Ida Hernandez Hayward, Lisa Fuller, Bronwyn Harris, Sneh Victoria Schnabel, Suzanne Grogan, and Sally De Spain. Thank you Trisha Nelson for sharing your touch, and thank you Joanna Lynne for sharing the heart behind the lens. My thanks to Patricia Hansen and Maureen Wallace for serving as honest midwives in this process.

Laurie O'Connell and Ed Barger, your professionalism and generosity made all the difference.

Thank you to the folks at Llumina Press for understanding dreams.

I am grateful that "Carrying Treasure" came so that I could thank my father, Ron Mason, my brothers: Fredrick Kay, Brian Martin, Timothy Scean and Thomas Christian, my uncles, my wonderful nephews, and Stanley Allen Boring, Dr. Lon Hatfield and Gregory D. Sharp, because you are the birds who helped me to finish my basket. Thank you.

This book is written especially out of love for Gabe.

FEATHER MEDICINE
Table of Contents

1

MARY

She combed her long black hair. The smell of wood smoke circled around the echo of her dream. In her dream she had seen her son. He was wounded, shot, unconscious, traveling into her dream world to tell her that he was alive. He was across the ocean but he was alive. She did not know fully what it meant, but she stood in the quiet of knowing that her son was not dead.

There were chickens to feed. As she wrapped hair ringlets around the curling iron that she pulled from the wood stove, firm curls encircled her high cheekbones. Wrapping one long braid in a circle around the back of her head, she took a deep breath. Breathing in the smell of early fall frost and wood walls, she braced herself for the day. It had been "one of those dreams." She knew she would need to be ready to hold it.

More wood in the stove, wrought iron skillets lifted onto the flat metal top, she began to cook. She listened to the early noises begin in the rest of the house: the shuffle of boots, men coughing, water being poured into the metal pan. All the men were waking. All the men who had come into the world through her body, and the slower, solid sounds of the man who had put them there.

Melting lard into the pan she listened to the greeting of the "hiss" when she poured in her chopped potatoes. She began another skillet with cool skinny sage hen wings, and breasts, and legs. Covering the skillets she went outdoors and began to feed the chickens. She liked the song that she and the chickens made. Her calling "here chick, chick," more often singing to them in her own language, the birds humming a response, she was efficient, but she fully listened to every note. This was the first song of her day and she always took the time to hear it.

Mary Bates was *Newe*. (That's what the Shoshoni people called themselves.) She, as all her people, was a child of the Coyote. He and his family sang her to sleep at night, and she told Coyote's stories as easily as she breathed. Putting a rock on the top fold of the chicken feed bag she opened the screen door and slipped her muddy boots off. The smell of breakfast was warm in the house and the men were beginning to mill around the table.

As she carried the plates and skillets to the table where the men all sat, creaks of wood chairs and the quiet laughter barely invaded her review of the dream. What had the location looked like? In the first part of her dream, definitely her son was bleeding. She was certain that the injury was serious. The second part of the dream was sterile, quiet, calm, and there was lots of white. She knew that it was not the afterworld because things were too neat. Everything was in order. Silver things lay in rows. Floors were shiny, and there was not the comfort that she encountered in her dreams of the dead.

She flowed like water through the breakfast. Gently moving this plate, that pan, pouring cold water in glasses, bringing coffee that had been boiled on the stove, the unobtrusive stream of a woman, quietly washing through the room of her men, unnoticed, but felt, at every turn.

The young men at the table were her sons. Two had already been to war. One had a woman leave him while he was overseas; she had sold his many cattle, and left him confused. He had actually been confused even before she left.

When he heard that there was a war, he had been willing to enlist. He went the 100 miles off the Reservation to the nearest recruiting office and they told him that he could not enlist because he did not have a birth certificate. He went home puzzled. They said he did not have the right paper. He had never been born.

He returned to the recruiting office after talking with a number of people at home. He had been born. Two of the Tribal Council members said they would write letters that he could take with him. They would write, and sign their names to documents, which would tell the United States Military Recruiter that the man standing in front of them had been born. They were sure that it would help him be able to go to war. The family had had many warriors. It would not be a new thing. He had been born a warrior. The second time at the recruiting office the men in uniform told him that maybe he had been born a warrior, but he had not been born a U.S. citizen. American Indians were not granted citizenship until 1924 and that was after he was born so it was just as if a Nazi had walked into the recruiting office and wanting to serve in the U.S. Army. He had not been born a U.S. citizen.

This had been his family's country forever. Some stories said that his family had been placed here by the hand of the Creator. His family had been here since the Creator placed people on the continent but he had not been born into the "country."

He went to a haystack and sat. He chewed on a sweet piece of straw and thought. While he was thinking Bull Eagle came up with a jug of wine. He told Bull Eagle that he wanted to defend the land of his people. He told him about the trip to town and how he had never been born and, then, how he had discovered that he had no more right to join the service than a Jerry or a Jap…(that's what they were calling people then…just like he knew he would almost always be called an "Engine").

He and Bull Eagle talked politics and drank until the bottle was empty. Then, they got in Bull Eagle's old truck and headed to town. They got another jug on the way, to continue the discussion, and when they got to town they both squinted to make out the letters on the window that said: "U.S. Army Recruiting Office".

The two men walked into the recruiter's office. They were big and brown and had hair that looked like licorice. It was stiff and black and shiny. The little pale man at the desk stayed calm as they both told him with 90 proof breath that they had certainly been born, and that they were from the people that the Creator had placed on the ground where he now stood.

The little pale man did not have as many rules as the first recruiter had and he, willingly, enlisted both of them. Bull Eagle later won a Purple Heart but he always swore that he did not even remember signing up.

This son who now sat at Mary's table had already been to war. When he came home from the recruiter's office and told her that he was going, she listened. She listened to the air and her heart and the spirits, and she knew that her fears for him did not need to start until he returned from war; that would be the time for him. Days later another son went into the service and a few more days later, yet another son signed up.

She was calm every day that her two sons at the table were in the war. Neighbors would ask her if she was worried, and she would tell them that she did not need to worry for these two sons while they were at war. One of her sons who now sat at the table, she did not need to worry about until he got home.

She noticed that the rhythm at the table was changing. The men were putting their coffee cups down with finality. They were ready to go feed. The chairs started to slide from under the table one by one.

It was time to tell them. "Your brother is alive. I dreamed him. I could see that he was hurt but you should know that he is alive. He needs to know that he is not alone. So, let him know that you see him."

Her statement came as easily as eating the sage hen. The brothers had a low rumbled agreement, and they each put a hand on her shoulder as they left the room.

The week was ordinary. Sky and ice and crispy grasses all brushed the legs and arms of the family. Then the letter came to the post office. Raymond James held the letter in his brown hand for some time. He thought about putting it in Mary's box. He looked at it; it was from the Department of War. He had never had one come in but he knew that it was important. It was the kind of letter that came when something bad had happened. It felt heavier than the paper it was made of.

Raymond knew that he was an agent of the United States Government. The Post Office Man was supposed to walk between the people and the government. Raymond was like an ambassador. Sometimes Raymond was tempted to walk in the power that he had rather than the kindness he had been born with. This time he was sure about where he had to walk.

Raymond locked up the post office and went out to the horse he had tied to the tree in the back of the post office. The bay gelding gave him one interested look as he grabbed the reins, and started to walk even as Raymond threw his leg over the saddle. Maybe the Indian Agent was the only person who would be upset that he had left his post. Anyone else would know that once he had held the letter, he had no choice.

Raymond walked the horse down the dirt road toward Mary's place. He thought about going at a gallop. Ten years ago, that was probably what he would have done. Now he knew that time did not matter. When something very tragic happened, sometimes it was better not to hurry with the news. He began to sing for Mary and her family. He prayed that they would all be strong. He prayed that Ellis, who the letter was most likely about, had a smooth trip over to the other side. He told Ellis that he would see him later and that he would be there for his mother. He talked with all of the relatives that he already had on the other side and he asked them to make Ellis comfortable. He asked Ellis to care for them as well. He sang without interruption for the ten miles of dirt road.

Mary was taking ice-cold laundry off of the clothesline when she heard the singing. She stopped, and she stood and she felt her dream coming. She took the clothes in her arms into the house, and then she walked out to the front road and waited for the dream to come. Bits of the song touched her ears long before she saw Raymond and his horse. With each touch of the song she breathed in the calm of her dream. It was a death song.

As she listened to the song she remembered that her son was alive and she did not take it in. Mary pulled her sweater closer to her and was glad for the dream.

Raymond and his horse walked slowly up to Mary. Raymond dismounted and handed the letter to Mary with the kindness he had been born with. "Here's a letter Mary. It's from the Government. Most likely it's about Ellis." For some of the other women on the Reservation, Raymond would have had to read the letter and then he would be sure what the letter said. But Mary knew how to read.

Ellis waited. He was sure she would open the letter, or begin to wail, or ask him to come in, but she just held it. She held the letter and felt her dream, and she knew that whatever was in the letter did not matter. As her body listened to the letter, she noticed Raymond and realized that he had come all this way and risked his job out of his kindness. She had to give him something.

"Let me get you a piece of pie," she said to him. She took the letter and left him standing with his horse while she went into the house to get his pie. Raymond was torn between thinking about Mary's pie and the letter. Mary made the best pie on the Reservation. Not everyone had such a gift. Big Sally was very generous with her pie but it had a crust that felt like wood. She was good-natured and her family thought that was the way pie was supposed to be. Even with the laughter that always came with Big Sally's pie, it was still hard to get down. The crunch-crunch of the crust was so loud that a person had a hard time hearing the taste over the crunch-crunch of the crust.

Sometimes, on top of the crunch-crunch, a person would run into a flour rock. Everyone would laugh when the lucky person would gingerly suck the rock loose from the crunchy crust. A standard phrase with Big Sally's pie was, " I almost broke a tooth!" Mary's pie was a different story. She had learned to make pie from white people and some people said she probably dreamed how to make the pies better. Some women secretly thought that was like cheating but when anyone ate her pie they didn't care where she learned it.

Raymond hoped that it was apple.

After Raymond had eaten his pie, Mary thanked him for coming. She knew not to disturb someone when they were tasting. She had just made the apple pie that morning and she knew it was Raymond's favorite, so she did not want to interrupt him with his old friend. When he was mounting up, she told him that she had dreamed Ellis. She knew the letter that came from the War Department was bad but Ellis was fine. Raymond told her he was glad to hear that Ellis was okay. Part of Raymond wished he had known that before he rode out; the other part of him was especially glad that he had found apple pie waiting for him.

When all the men came in from the field for lunch, Mary told them a letter had come from the War Department. She guessed it was about Ellis but she said there was not really any reason to read it because of her dream. All the men ate their lunch, occasionally glancing at the letter unopened on the table corner.

As they were leaving, one of the brothers who had already been to war grabbed the letter. Everyone pretended not to notice it. When he stepped outside he opened the envelope gingerly and read: Ellis was missing in action.

Things went on the way they do. The damp smell of fall turned into the frozen horse trough. Snow came; there was more rumbling of men in the house now than there had been in the summer. A big mule deer needed to be dressed out, and the smell of venison mixed with the wood smoke.

The letter continued to lie on Mary's kitchen counter, and soon the discussion about the letter died down in town. Everyone knew about Mary's dream and about how Raymond had ridden all the way out to the Bates' place because no one had bothered to tell him about the dream. The story always did rightly include the apple pie at the end and everyone assumed that perhaps that was the reason the letter had come. Raymond needed pie.

Late in the spring a strange vehicle came into town. Two men in uniform asked at the little post office where Mary Bates lived, Mary, who was the mother of Ellis. The entire town breathed differently. There were no telephones but dust trails and the looks in people's faces, and the air, told everyone that something had happened.

Two men arrived in Mary's yard. When Mary heard the automobile pull up, for some reason she thought about Ellis. She told him in her heart that she knew that he was alive and she looked out the window to see who was there.

When Mary saw the two men getting out of the car she checked her coffee pot to make sure there was enough for two guests. Fortunately, she had made two pies that morning, one was cherry and the other was apricot. She went into the food room, opened the pie drawer, and took both pies out. She cut one large slice of each and put them on plates on the table. She just had time, after she placed their forks, to walk to the door to greet the men.

Mary opened the screen door. The boys looked nervous and serious. She knew that they were grown but they were younger than some of her own children, so she could not help but think of them as boys. Both were in uniform. It was clear they had made an effort to arrive looking official and respectful. Mary smiled to try to make them more comfortable. They were both white. She could guess that neither had been on a Reservation before but that was not what made them nervous. Her reassuring voice, "Come in, come in" that sounded something like her chick-chick song, seemed to make them more uncomfortable. She thought she saw the beginning of a tear on the eye of the taller one.

She wanted to spare them discomfort; she knew they were there about her dream. "Come sit and have some pie. I just made it this morning. My sons and my husband are out working in the fields, they're busy with hay. Two of my sons have come back from the service. One got malaria and the other got yellow fever. Imagine, we have all sorts of mosquitoes around the irrigation ditches and they never got anything. Being away from home, they even had a hard time with mosquitoes. One of my other sons is away in Europe, I don't exactly know where, but I know that he's alive. His sisters and I knitted hundreds of socks this past winter for him and other boys who were getting cold feet. Maybe one of you got some of the socks?"

The two men in uniform looked at each other with dread. The shorter one stood straighter as he said, "Ma'am, that's why we're here. It's in regard to your son." The serious young man held out a piece of rectangular metal with a tin colored chain strung through it. "It is my sad duty to inform you that your son, Ellis, was killed in action. He died in combat saving the lives of many other men in his platoon. Therefore, we wish to give you, on his behalf, this Purple Heart and his dog tags, which were found at the scene of the battle." The tall boy pulled a beautiful box out from inside his jacket and they both held their items toward her, sad that she had won such a prize.

Mary looked at both of them. Both children, both wanting so much to be prepared to calm her as they wished someone would do for their mothers in the event the same news had to be given some day. She looked at both of them and smiled and said, "Come sit down and have some pie now."

The men looked at each other, startled. They wondered if Mary was in shock. They had been given some preparation regarding how parents and families might react when they brought such news, but honestly, they had expected that shock would at least include a shocked look…or a gasp, or a pause, but they had come a long way. Mary was calm and welcoming, and the pie beckoned them both.

It was as though each piece of pie had a name card. There was no debate or hesitation. Each knew immediately which piece of pie belonged to them, and which chair to sit in. When they sat and became absorbed in the pie, the room became familiar and they chewed and listened while Mary told them about her dream. The taller young man told her that he was from the Louisiana swamps and he had always heard about things like that. He told her that if her dream was true, he was glad her son was not dead. She noticed how he sang when he talked, not quite like an Indian but it was still a song.

The other young man was visibly irritated to hear his partner feed her fantasy. He took pains to explain that Ellis had been with a platoon, and he had seen a grenade. He had flung himself on the grenade to protect the men around him. Ellis's dog tags had blown off and the same had happened to the tags of several other soldiers around him. When they picked up the body parts and tags, they knew who they had to contact. Until they had found all the dog tags, they just had a bunch of M.I.A.'s. The Swamp Man was uncomfortable with the presentation and, were it not for that, he would have loved to accept a second piece of pie.

"Your son served his country well," said the serious man.

"Just a minute boys, wait right here." Mary went into the food room and looked at her pies. She pulled out two paper bags and folded them until they were stiff. She put half of each pie on each of the bags. She knew the pie would be gone before they were out of town. She thought about giving them forks but she knew her pie held up just right being eaten by hand.

She came out of the food room and handed each of them their pie. The Swamp Man looked at her enthusiastically and said, "Ma'am, I'm sorry we're bearin' bad news but, I wanna tell you, this is the best cherry pie I've had since my Mom's. We have a tree out back at home and I can hardly wait each year, till those cherries get right. I imagine I'll be pickin' those cherries for her when I'm 70, just to be sure I get my pie. I thank ya!" With that, the singing Swamp Man reached down and hugged her enthusiastically. She was surprised. The official man was furious, but the Swamp Man walked out on a cloud with his cherry pie.

In the dust, as the vehicle pulled out, Mary saw her dream, and she saw her son, wounded, and alive.

Several months passed, and there was no word from Ellis. One of the sons who had come back from the war felt that the dog tags, and the box with the Purple Heart, over-rode the dream. There was discussion in the town. Some wanted to wish Mary condolences, have a potluck, and have some wailing; those who knew enough to be wailers would have no part of it. They knew that Mary's dream was the final authority.

Months past, and Mary dreamed again. In the dream Mary saw all the white and she saw her son being moved. He was put in a big box-like rig and driven through her dream to another building that was filled with people dressed in white. She looked at her son. He was covered with bandages but she could feel him, and she could feel him getting stronger. Then in her dream she saw him lift a bandaged hand. She saw him point his finger and she saw him lay his finger down hard on a metal button. She did not know what it meant but she could feel his determination. When Mary woke, she felt better than she had felt since the Swamp Man left.

Many weeks later a letter arrived from France. In the letter a nurse explained that Mary's son, Ellis, had been seriously wounded. Apparently, he had thrown himself on a live granade to protect others in his platoon. Although his body had taken the bulk of the blast, shrapnel scattered in every direction and others were killed. A land mine had gone off close to where Ellis had been standing. Dog tags, wounded, and the "missing" were difficult to assess. Ellis had been unconscious for months; when he regained consciousness he was unable to speak. Though still in serious condition, he was stabilized, and then moved to the French hospital where he would receive rehabilitation until he could be shipped home. The nurse explained that part of his rehabilitation involved learning to type, to restore his coordination and to allow him to communicate. She indicated that a letter that he had typed was enclosed.

Years later, when Mary died, the letter was found in a floral cookie tin under her bed.

The typed letter read:

I am alive.

Ellis

Mary never had to explain her "knowing." In her community, it was as accepted as the migration of geese and the connection of children to their Grandparents. It was often as welcome as rain on the dry sagebrush. Mary had a gift. It was her gift but it was there for her family, and many times for her entire community.

Mary's people had always been dreamers. These dreamers were not viewed as sacred although, sometimes, the information they were allowed to carry was. They each had their weaknesses and their human frailty, but they also had their dreams. Never did anyone think to interrogate, or doubt, or mock. It was just so.

2

ANNIE

Annie's mother was Shoshone and her Grandmother, Mary, was a dreamer. Annie's father was white and she lived in a city that had languages and colors and smells in abundance. There were phrases that her mother used with the babies that she bore, which were not in English. There was the rock that her mother heated in the electric oven and wrapped with a towel when one of the kids had an ear ache. When Annie saw the little flat heating pad at a friend's house, she knew that one of them was different. Either it was her friend, whose Grandma wore wooden shoes and spoke little English, or it was she. Between the two of them, it didn't really matter.

Annie's other friend, Lupita, had a mother and a Grandmother in her home who spoke another language as well. Annie would watch in fascination, as the Grandma would comb Lupita's hair. She would pull her long black hair into a tight braid making Lupita look slightly oriental because she would braid her hair so tightly. When the Grandma was finished combing, all the while speaking rapidly in her other language, she would quickly cut a tomato in half and swipe the open half all around Lupita's head. She would take care to pick out any lingering tomato seeds and by the time Annie and Lupita would get to school, the tomato juice had dried to a stiff sheen. Annie knew that no one in her own family put tomato on their hair but she admired the way it made Lupita's hair look newly combed all day long.

Annie's mother had brown eyes and warm hands with smooth fingernails. Mother's hands were always busy guiding, stroking, patting, holding. Annie was the first of seven children within eleven years so the holding and touching hands were like dancers who were forever involved in the joy of the dance. It was not until Annie was a woman herself that she could reflect on her mother's eyes and see that at times the woman had been tired. As a child, all she felt and saw were the warm brown hands.

All of the children were different colors. Once, a man from Morocco explained how, when he was a child, all of the colors of the people in his family were described as honey. There was light honey, golden honey, and dark honey. Annie thought it was a wonderful characterization of all of the shades that are seen in honey and people alike. Annie loved the luminescence of that description and she saw clearly that all of the hues of honey were represented in her and in her siblings.

Annie's father had blue eyes. All her relatives, except her father, had brown eyes, and so somehow, she was amazed by her father's eyes. She remembered thinking to ask him once what had happened to his eyes. They glittered with love but she wondered if it had hurt when he had the color taken out and she wondered how old he had been when it happened. She never actually asked because she somehow sensed that it might hurt his feelings. She never asked and, eventually, she no longer wondered about it.

Her father was a pocket full of lemon drops. Annie loved walking beside her father, and she loved the times that he would invite her to reach into his coat pocket and take a lemon drop. Sometimes the lemon drops were covered with lint; she would walk and talk with him, discretely spitting lint as they walked and talked.

As a young woman Annie once found herself picking lint off of a sweater and salivating. She laughed when she realized that holding the lint had brought the taste of lemon to her memory's tongue.

Given the diversity around her, Annie was sure that she and her family were the norm. Then the family moved to a rural area which was much less diverse and, suddenly, the family, except for Dad, was definitely Indian. People often wanted to hear her mother speak Shoshone but their insistence and persistence somehow felt like children who wanted to see a six-legged frog.

There was not the variety of colors and sounds in the small town but the mountains surrounding them were beautiful. There was the stability of parochial school where no murmurings were heard about origins. Most of the teens in the Catholic school had parents or Grandparents who spoke a foreign language.

Life was full of study, laughter, watching her brothers' baseball games, horseback riding, and visiting her Grandmother on the reservation in the summer time. Time with her Grandmother infused Annie with a deep sense of belonging. The chores and laughing were so connected to the stories, and the stories to dreams, and all was somehow not separate from her.

At times she felt like a happy observer. This was her life.

In the summer, Annie would go to help with the hay. When the alfalfa fields were covered with a delicate veil of lavender, the alfalfa was ready to cut. After helping Grandma with breakfast, Annie would run out in the field to start the tractor. Cousins, brothers, and Uncles would surround the tractor and wooden trailer bed. Each adjusting their gloves, their hats, some looking at the hills in the distance, some looking at the hayfield, another checking the tractor hoses and hitches before beginning the day. Annie would start the tractor.

She sat on the cold metal seat, above her Uncles, but she did not feel bigger, and she always felt very protected.

One of her Uncles had been a paratrooper in Korea, another had been a combat veteran in the European Theatre. One of the Uncles had been in the service in Burma, and the other had been in the Philippines. One had yellow fever, another had malaria, and still another had a scar that covered three quarters of his torso. They never talked about it and they moved as one man when it was time to hay.

As the brothers moved, Annie often felt someone else. At times she thought she felt a place for the eldest brother, the Uncle who had died in prison. He had been a handsome man of fine features, who had been multi-lingual. He had spoken Shoshone, Paiute, Spanish, English, and maybe other languages. He traveled, he was brown, and he was intelligent. He was one of those Indian men at that certain time. His intellect and social stereotype could never meet. He was lost but he often appeared when all of the brothers were together. He did not need to be visible to be there. He had come first and he had left first.

Annie remembered her mother talking about the only time she had seen him, when she was a young girl; he was the eldest brother. She had been shy, and he was there at home on the Reservation for so short a time. Yet, when he sat at the kitchen table, and she stood nearby, she felt connected to him, her brother. Because Annie's mother, Mona, had told the story and shared the feeling of her brother, Annie recognized the presence of her invisible Uncle, beautiful and sure, whenever all of her Uncles stood together.

When they all hayed, all the brothers, the cousins, and Annie driving the old John Deere, Annie would find the rhythm. With the tractor humming its way through the alfalfa field, Annie learned not to go too slow for all the men who were loading bales onto the hay-bed. As the afternoon became hotter, she learned not to wear anyone out. She would slow down as the day got hotter, without making any of her manly, adolescent cousins with their new muscles appear weak. Annie didn't laugh out loud when she saw her skinniest cousin roll up his t-shirt sleeves, to give both the world and himself a better look at the muscles on his arms that looked like the foreleg of a skinned doe.

Annie learned not to go too fast for the men as they began to sweat. She learned to let the tractor walk with the men in her family. She learned to let the tractor pull the trailer bed at exactly the pace the men needed. Annie learned to *feel* her Uncles, cousins, and brothers.

3

NE TOKO: MY GRANDPA

Annie remembered sitting outside with her Grandpa. The ground was dry and the big cottonwoods covered the two of them like an umbrella. His hands were the hands that had cleared land, milked cows, and signed Tribal documents. Grandpa's hands had driven teams of horses for the stage that brought supplies to the reservation, held books and children, and grandchildren, and great-grandchildren. As he and Annie sat together, breathing the same air, side by side, she often looked at his powerful, gentle hands. The tip of one of Grandpa's fingers was gone.

He was very old. One winter, late in his life, he had been chopping wood, as he had for decades, and one hand forgot what that regular rhythm, the song and the dance of wood-chopping went like. So, one brisk morning when he looked at the split wood, part of the new-cut wood was red with blood.

Annie would sit beside her Grandpa for hours. Most often they sat in quiet. They were both at peace in the song of the magpies taunting each other and they would sometimes break the silence by laughing together. They could sit together and watch an ant carry the body of another insect, for what must have been in the insect world, hundreds of miles. The little ant persisted, for the sake of family, out of some agreement with life. The ant would consistently do what appeared could not be done. As her Grandpa sat with her, watching the ant, she knew that she was learning.

Unspoken as it was, part of the sitting was a challenge. Who could be still, who could be in quiet, the longest. At times, they would each go for an hour or more, and when they were done, when Grandpa would begin to get up to go back into the house, they both went in knowing that they had shared. They sat together, in the quiet, on the land, with the same blood drumming in their veins, as they sat for the desert's song.

In sitting quietly beside her grandfather, sometimes nature had the opportunity to entertain. Once, as she and her grandfather sat side by side in the dry blue-sky day, a small gray bird landed on the dusty ground in front of them. The little bird pecked vigorously at the few seeds the chickens had ignored that morning. Annie and her Grandpa sat. As often happened she could feel the sharing of their new shift in focus. With his little tail facing Annie and her Grandpa, the feather-covered, industrious worker became committed to gathering the downy white hair that was dancing in the dust every time a breeze came. The collie had left fluffy clumps every time he scratched in celebration of spring. Annie and her Grandpa watched quietly as they saw the little bird's tail pop up again and again. When Annie made a small noise in her suppression of a giggle, the little bird turned with theatrical precision and all was lost as she and her Grandpa shared laughter that painted the valley. The little bird looked directly at them appearing, for all the world, like a little indignant old man, with a long flowing white beard shaking just below his beak.

Sometimes, after hours of sitting, Grandpa would give her a treasure: a story.

Most of the stories were about "we." When "we" went to Carlisle. When "we" say horse, "we" say *"punku."* When we say Grandpa, (your mother's father), we say *"Ne Toko"* (the word "I" was almost never used by the old people in story telling). All of the stories about "us" created a sense that these were her stories, too. Annie learned that she, too, would be a story one day. She lived as a story within the story. She knew that she was not the whole of the story; she was not alone in the tale. Annie's Grandparents had been in the story before she was and her great-Grandparents were in the story before them, and the story had started with the ancestors before them, all the way back to the beginning of the story, which started with Coyote.

Annie always listened when her Grandparents told the part of the story that was theirs.

"When we rode to Carlisle, Pennsylvania, on the train," Grandpa said, "you could see some people die on the train." There was an understanding that the death was of their spirit, not their physical body. The more Annie heard the stories, the more she felt them. She gradually learned to hear the part of the story that was not told in words. The part that was told in the far away looks, the anguish, (or the trickster) in the voice. Gradually, Annie would learn to hear the part of the story that was told by silence. The most powerful part of the story was told in the pause in the story, the nod, the moment in the story when the storyteller could not go on, and would begin to draw in the dust with a walking stick.

Sometimes Grandpa talked about Carlisle Indian School. "We thought this one young man was really uncoordinated, because he was always trying to jump over desks and anything else he could find. Sometimes he didn't make it. But we didn't know, then, that he was just practicing to be Jim Thorpe." When Grandpa said "we," Annie could see the slim, brown, young Thorpe jumping for all he was worth and her eyes laughed beside her Grandpa as she remembered it.

The story was for Annie. It didn't mean that Grandpa had been in Carlisle with Jim Thorpe; it didn't mean necessarily that Jim Thorpe had an awkward phase. The story was for Annie, and it simply meant, "Don't be afraid to jump. Don't expect to get it right the first time, and don't be discouraged if you don't make it the first time." Annie kept the story.

Sometimes, going back inside after sitting with Grandpa, Annie would help her Grandma make pies. She would cut the fruit, or grab the flour sack out of the pantry, put down the hot plates, or roll the dough. While they worked, sometimes Grandma Mary would tell a story. Some of the stories were meant for Annie to keep.

Annie kept the Water Baby story. It was a true story.

4

THE WATER BABIES

When Annie's Grandma Mary was a young woman, she and her family had to go up into the mountains for water. In those days, the irrigation ditches were not in. The little creek (which liked to be called a river) would dry up toward the end of the summer. So, families would have to get jugs, and saddle the horses, and everyone would set out, up into the hills to water the horses and get as much water as the horses could pack. To keep everyone comfortable, they would all camp for the night, tell stories, and laugh. Some would gather whatever little chokecherries hadn't dried up. No one knew what century it was. The same blood had come to these mountains for thousands of years. Ancestors had stood laughing in the same place and telling the same stories. Dressed in buckskin one century, and dressed in Levi's the next, the stories and the families didn't change.

Some of the stories were for entertainment. The story of the Water Babies was true. It is a true thing, even now, that young mothers have to be careful by the water with their small children. Older brothers and sisters too, have to be especially cautious. When older brothers or sisters watch younger siblings, the Water Babies may call, even in the day.

They are not mean, but it is true that they are there. The beings in the water are called "pa'ohaa"...the Water Babies. These Water Babies get lonely and in the night, or when there are not many people around, they will cry and call little children to come play with them in the water. The little children hear the voices of the

Water Babies, they feel their loneliness, and the little child will go into the water to comfort the Water Baby and the child will drown.

Mary told Annie about the time when she was a young mother herself, many years back, and her eyes went to that time as she told Annie about the Water Babies.

Grandma Mary told about hearing the Water Babies in the water, after the sun went down, one particular year when they had gone to the hills for water. Mary said that she had heard the Water Babies crying. Her youngest baby, a son, was still at her breast. Mary's body tightened as she told how restless her new baby became when he heard the cry of the Water Babies. She told how she held the little one with her body and her prayers, how all night she heard the little cry from the river, how all that night she tried to sooth the need of her little one to comfort the Water Babies. Mary told how hard she fought sleep, and how she felt such fear for her baby. Toward dawn, the day's ride caught up with her, and she knew that she could not stay awake.

Mary told Annie that this was her last baby that she held. She had experienced many years of children in her womb, at her breast and in her arms, and had much more experience than a new mother could have. She told Annie that she was so glad that she had cared for so many other children. She told Annie that any new mother would have certainly lost her child that night to the Water Babies.

Annie swallowed as Grandma Mary continued. Mary described how when she woke in the morning, she was clutching her baby son so tightly that he was struggling with her. She opened her eyes, and looked at his little black eyes, then smiled as she released her grip. Mary handed him a breast in reconciliation. She put her head on her hand as she rested on her elbow, lying there by the creek bed.

She had clung to her little one all night, even as she slept. And she imagined that the Water Babies had called to him all night, even as she slept.

As she began to allow her body to feel relief, she suddenly felt the wind surround her body with fear. She held her son tightly as he drank, and she looked at the little, tiny baby size footprints, facing the place where she, and her little one lay. She shuddered as she noticed the way the tracks nervously paced here and there and then, finally, headed back toward the water, alone.

The world was somehow different on the Reservation. Love even felt different. Love could be a house full of cowhides on the floor.

Every year when they branded which was done as a community, little leppy calves were found. These were the baby calves that had no mothers. Some of the calves were orphans. Others had just been born to a mother who did not want to feed them and care for them. No one said that such a cow was bad; it was just the way it was.

In the old days, Annie had heard mothers and babies had always been left to The Spirit. A young woman, in the old days, might give birth but not be called to be a mother. No one said she was bad. No child suffered while its mother was forced to mother when she had not been called to do so. What was known was that the birth was perfect. If the woman who bore the child did not hear a song that sang that she was a mother, the birth had happened for the sake of another, who was meant to be a mother and could not bear children or, perhaps, some woman who had lost a child and had many gifts for mothering. Everyone knew that it was exactly right when the baby went from birth to the mother for whom the child had been sent.

No one said, "Everyone who gives birth must be a mother." No one said, "If you have a child, and you are not called to be a mother, we will call that criminal. You may not just give your child to the one for whom the child was meant."

When the cows in the spring knew they were not mothers, it was because Annie's Auntie could never have enough children to use all her mother gifts. She had so much left over that the four-legged babies gave her a place for all her gifts.

5

LOVE HIDES

Every Spring Annie's Uncle and Aunt would take the leppy calves home to bottle-feed; and Annie's Aunt loved the leppies. She named them and talked to them when she fed them with giant-size baby bottles. She had half a dozen children that she would also assign to calf duty. In her heart there was something special about these little ones who had been left to die. The names of the calves reflected her affection: Baby, Chubby, Honey, Cookie…each spring a new list of loved baby calves could be heard being cuddled by Annie's Aunty's voice.

The thing was, after a spring and summer of nurturing confiding, it was time to butcher the calves. Every year, Annie's Auntie knew the fate of her calves but she could not help but weep when it was time for her babies to be slaughtered.

Annie's Uncle loved his wife in a quiet, solid way, in the way the mesa mountain stays on the ground. He loved the way that she cared for their children and he loved the way that she cared for the calves. He appreciated the way she cooked her beans and sometimes did things differently, like the time that she decided to cook lima beans and tomato, instead of sticking to the pinto beans like everyone else did. He knew that her driving tractor to help with the hay and her eye for good horses had made his life easier many times. He loved her, and he could not bear to do nothing when he saw her weep.

First, it was just the baby calf that was the most special, the original "Baby". Uncle had the hide fixed by a taxidermist in the next town, which was one hundred miles away. He took Baby's hide to the little taxidermy shop that had a sign written with black felt pen on poster board, taped to the front door. The sign said: "TAXES AND TAXIDERMY: TAXES PREPARED SO YOU DON'T HAVE TO HIDE! REMEMBER THAT HUNTING TRIP, LET US DO YOUR HIDE!" When the hide had been cured, Uncle gave it to the woman that he loved, to help her with her sorrow, and she was entirely soothed.

The following year, he took all of the hides of the leppy calves that she mourned for to the taxidermist. The end result was that by the time Annie was an adult, both stories of the house were floored with cowhides. Auntie knew each one by name, and still called each by name with as much affection as she had when they were living.

Where was the phone book? "Oh, it's upstairs in the drawer by "Baby." Where was the laundry? "Oh, it's in a basket downstairs by "Lovey."

Anyone who did not know the hides by name would be at a distinct disadvantage in Auntie's house when she needed to tell you where you could definitely find something. Auntie loved saying their names and Uncle loved that he had found a workable solution for her tears.

The soft brown and white pelts that covered the floors quietly said that there was love in this house.

6

THE FAMILY RECIPE

No one on the Reservation could cook like Mary. Part of the results had to do with the fact that Mary had a vegetable garden that was encompassed by hollyhocks. Her peas, beans and potatoes had been a part of a quiet oasis in the desert.

One man who came every year to help with the haying was a Frenchman. When Mary would be asked to introduce him, she would state, "This is the Frenchman."

The Frenchman clearly enjoyed good cuisine, as any Frenchman should.

Every year when it was time to put up hay, the Frenchman would appear. At times when other people on the reservation had difficulty getting their hay up, Mary's cooking encouraged people from the other end of the globe to come and help with the hay.

The Frenchman received tremendous respect when he came to help with Mary's hay. He knew good food and he worked very hard. The fresh salads that were lightly covered with Mary's simple blend of pepper, vinegar, oil and sugar apparently called the Frenchman to labor every year.

What Annie discovered years later was that the accent that was attributed to a Foreign Land was only the result of the "Frenchman" having been the genetic recipient of a "hare-lip." Even after the discovery, Annie had a sense that the reverence the "Frenchman" had for good cooking, and the loyalty that he had to Mary's family every year when they needed to put up their hay, was all that really mattered.

Annie understood. When she took a friend, years later, to the Reservation, she introduced the loyal, stocky man as "The Frenchman."

When Annie was on the Reservation, she realized that "story" was as important as breath. The stories were the places where the ancestors and the children met, and played, and cried, and began to experience the understanding of what it meant not to ever be separated. They shared blood and they shared stories; both absolutely represented the continuation of life.

When Annie was little, her Grandmother told her that once there was a little girl who had been just about the same age as Annie.

The little girl had heard about a magic place. It was a small house that had all kinds of paper that was put together to make books. In the "books" were the stories of everything that had ever happened in the world. This little girl was soooo excited. (Every word sounded like song when Annie's Grandmother told the story.) The little girl loved stories, and so she decided in herself that she would go, she would go into the building, and she would learn the magic of the books.

The little girl thought about it all night, so excited she could hardly sleep. She knew that as soon as she woke up she was going to go to the place and present herself and her love of stories. Her heart was right. Her world would change.

The little girl woke up early. Her heart was pounding as she jumped up, got dressed and headed for the building. When she arrived, the other children who were there looked surprised. An adult came over to her and told her that she would have to leave. "You can't come in here. You're Indian."

She walked out of the wooden building and away from the grown-up who told her she did not belong there with her back straight and her head up. As she walked down the steps, and away from the school, tears came to her eyes making the world blur. The little girl walked home on the dirt road. Her tears almost blinded her to the point that she didn't see the Coyote droppings in the middle of the road. As the little girl sobbed, she walked around Coyote's droppings, she remembered that she had a choice about where she walked no matter what she encountered on the road.

Annie's Grandmother whispered, "That little girl was this old lady you see here. That little girl was your Grandma." As she said those words, there was the shadow of the tears of the little girl who was told to leave the school, and Annie cried. Her Grandmother laughed gently, smoothed Annie's hair and said, "But I taught *myself* to read." (She was a voracious reader.) "And every time you go to school, you can go for that little girl who became your Grandma."

So it was, that when Annie studied, when she read everything she possibly could, she knew that she was making the world right.

7

MILLIE

In her early teens, Annie began to discover something powerful. She discovered that if she and her friends wrapped their arms and breasts around the priest's arms when they walked in the school hallway with him, his faced turned the most unusual crimson and he would sweat. They noticed that if they asked him questions about religion as they did this, he would get one single, deep wrinkle in between his eyebrows as he struggled to stay in the conversation. As they giggled and squeezed him he would become more crimson, and the wrinkle would become deeper, until he would smile nervously and excuse himself hurriedly, always parting with a shaky voice that encouraged them to continue to ask questions.

Annie noticed that when the bus was crowded on the way to the basketball games, if she wiggled in the lap of one of the players, they would get a lump in their pocket. Something about that made her feel very playful.

Her mother watched her, and that summer when she went to the Reservation her Auntie Millie picked her up at the bus station. Auntie Millie was strong and very beautiful. She knew how to shoot but she always let her men hunt. She wore perfectly ironed blouses and always drove a new car. She chewed Doublemint gum that she bought in industrial sized bags because she believed in a bargain, and she used even her gum to full advantage. Most people would just chew gum lazily. Millie used it as punctuation. She would end a sentence with pregnant silence, laughter or, when in need of emphasis, she would end her sentence with a "snap", making her gum sound just like an exclamation point. Sometimes it would sound like a question mark. And sometimes, when she told a story and wanted a magical pause, she would blow a little gray bubble. She said big pink bubbles were rude, but little gray, minty, fresh bubbles were fine for a lady.

Annie knew there was some reason that Millie had come to pick her up. It just felt like there was something important in that. Millie looked at her. She could feel her Aunt looking her up and down, looking in her heart and looking at her hair, looking like she would at a horse that she was going to buy, seeing its speed with the horse still standing. Millie chuckled in her throat.

Millie was always fun. She ran the kitchen in the Reservation hospital and she knew how to heal people with food. Whenever Annie got to wash her hands and cook with her, Millie would recite all kinds of information about the healing in food, the vitamins, the fats, the minerals, the colors, the textures, and ultimately, the love and the beauty. Annie learned from her to turn radishes and celery leaves into bouquets of roses. She would slice down the sides from the top of the radish to the bottom, four or five times, stopping just before cutting the radish skin off making perfect red petals. Then she learned to make a little cross on the top of the radish, making it look as though the whole rose had not yet bloomed. The most exciting thing was to see the little radish rose sitting on top of a celery leaf tip; it looked so much like a proud little flower.

Millie was well known for being a cooking healer and her work at the hospital had an impact in the community. When someone had to be taken to the hospital, sometimes even before the questions regarding how the surgery went, someone would ask the recovering patient, "What did you have to eat?"

Annie looked at her, and her Auntie laughed. "So, you're discovering boys!" Annie looked at her Aunt's acceptance and she smiled shyly. Millie smiled and then snapped her gum several times as though she were winding up her mouth to say what she had decided to say.

Millie was ready to claim all the space in the car and all the space in the desert around them as she taught Annie something. "I'm going to tell you something, Annie"(snap). Annie listened with all her being because her Auntie was giving her something that was just for her.

"There's something you need to know" (snap, snap). "There are enough peters to go around this world twice so you don't ever have to be in a hurry to get yours." (Perfect, slow, gray, minty bubble.)

Millie did not say another word all the 50 miles to the Reservation. Annie sat quietly in amazement. She felt entirely comfortable and excited and utterly content with the picture her Auntie had just given her. And she felt as though it was two women who were riding home in Aunt Millie's car.

Something about Auntie Millie's information gave Annie an incredible calm. It also helped her to define, once again, differences between the two camps that she could move back and forth between. In the Native American camp, people had genitals. In the white camp, they did not. In the Shoshone stories, the animals had sexual relations and temptations and laughed when they had intercourse. In the white stories, there were animals, but they were usually so much more separate from the people. You could have black birds that you baked in a pie, or black sheep, or fat hogs, but the animals had never been people and they did not have as much to teach. Annie knew that in Catholic school she could not tell her friends about how Coyote could even disguise himself as a man to have sex with them. But then, since the white girls did not have genitals, maybe Coyote would not have been interested.

8

TWO WORLDS

There were times when the presence of the two worlds led to temporary confusion. Like the time a bird flew into their living room in their home in the white suburbs. Instantly, Annie's mother's face was full of anxiety as she grabbed a broom in one swift movement and began to holler at all of her children to "Get that bird out of the house!!" She leapt and swung and her children looked at their usually composed mother in amazement. Her sense of urgency was unsettling but intoxicating at the same time.

After a stunned pause, her young sons realized that they were being given carte blanche to swing and jump and holler. Paperback books and plastic cups and couch cushions began to fly around the room as they all yelled and jumped, almost forgetting that the object was to oust the bird.

After an eternity of young brown legs and arms flying in every direction with enthusiasm, the bird flew out the front door. The room looked as though a tornado had hit. Books, couch cushions, dish towels, a green and yellow polka-dot stuffed animal boa constrictor, and even a bag of M&M candy that had scattered across the floor lay in stunned quiet; the silence was coupled with concern for Annie's mom. As definitely as she had leapt to her feet, she now looked sincerely worried. Chaos and anxiety were two things that rarely occurred when Annie's mother was anywhere in the vicinity, let alone occurring as a result of her distress.

The room was deadly calm as all the brown eyes looked at Annie's mom. The experience was surreal.

With one little bead of sweat glittering under her nose, Annie's mom tried to look composed. "It's bad luck to have a bird in the house."

Immediately, having all their questions answered, her sons, who all admired deductive reasoning and logic, competed to assuage her fears.

"Oh! Is that all it is… that was just for tee pees. This house was not built by Indians so that does not apply to this house! That was just for the tee pees because they were so small that if a bird flew in, *someone* would get hit by bird shit."

One of the younger brothers, not quite as confident, looked at his mother's anxious eyes and spoke up to defend her fears, "This house has Indians in it, so this is an Indian house! If a bird flies into an Indian house, it *is* bad luck."

"Is not!"

"Is too!"

"Is not!"

"Is too!"

Suddenly, Annie's mother remembered that, first, she was the mother and she interrupted, "You boys stop that and go play outside. First pick up all the things you threw and then go out and play catch for a while." And as she walked out of the living room Annie heard her say under her breath, "It's too late now. It already flew in."

There were, occasionally, other things that reminded Annie that her family was unique. Some were big, and some were as small as a wasp stinger.

Once, during the 4th of July Rodeo and Pow Wow, Annie sat on a wasp. The wasp retaliated and Annie ran with the twinge of pain to her mother to tell her what had happened. Her mother was sitting with her own sisters, Annie's Aunts, all of them lined up like judges on the edge of the rodeo arena.

When Annie reported what had happened, her eldest Aunt said, "Put snot on it. That will take the poison out."

Annie was disgusted but for the rest of the day she encountered cousins, Uncles, and other interested community members who would say with authority, "I heard you got stung. Did you put snot on it?"

She guessed that if she were any other place on the planet, that would not be the immediate response she would get over a bee sting. But it was good that here, everyone knew the same cure. And Annie knew that had she been stung several times, rather than just once, she might even have tried it.

She knew that the old remedies worked. She remembered once seeing one of the little ones with a badly infected hangnail. His little sausage shaped finger was puffy and hot. They were visiting another area for a Pow Wow. One of the Indian Elder women saw the painful little finger, and she picked a Wormwood leaf. She boiled a small pan of water and placed the leaf in the water. The entire time, she told the little one a story about some tremendous cure that had been wrought by the little herb. She took the leaf out of the pan with a spoon.

As she laid the leaf on a clean washcloth, the little one was hypnotized with fascination. The Elder peeled away the stringy vein on the back side of the leaf and lay that side down on the little one's finger, gently wrapping the warm leaf around it.

He looked up at her and they both smiled when she told him, "Now we wait."

Annie lost interest after several minutes of watching old age and youth grinning at each other, but when she saw the little one the following day she could not tell which finger had been sore. He came up to Annie and said, "The Grandma and Wormwood fixed my finger." And that was true.

Annie knew that her mother could stop an aching gland. She would heat a big flat river rock in the electric oven. When the rock was as warm as it used to be when it watched the sun all day, her mother would wrap it with a towel. She remembered watching her mother rubbing her hand first over the smooth rock...soothing the rock? Soothing herself? Definitely soothing Annie.

Her mother would stroke the smooth, flat, gray river rock with her silken caramel hand, and then she would put it in the oven to heat. When the rock was heated, her mother would wrap the rock in a big towel and place it under Annie's head, just behind her ear where her gland was swollen. The rock (even with the towel) was hard, but it was warm. She never knew what happened next because the few times she felt ill enough for her mother to use the rock, she fell asleep with the rock singing to her. All she remembered was a warm healing song and her mother's smooth hand stroking the rock.

She had often wished that dating had a bigger place in her world. There was always homework to be done. Many of her friends had been dating since their early teens. For Annie, a date meant taking one of her many brothers and sisters, or several of them, wherever some unsuspecting young man got her parent's permission to take her.

At seventeen, in her senior year, Annie was finally able to have an unsupervised date. Before, her siblings had to accompany her, severely limiting the possible outcomes of every date she'd had. Her parents had to agree upon a responsible prospect and finally gave her the opportunity to have an actual date.

The lucky winner was a guy she had known throughout her adolescence. He was older than she, had a shiny new red pickup, had just started college, wore Pendleton shirts, and smelled good.

The two of them had gone to a movie and now, he was parking his brand new truck. He looked at her, and she closed her eyes. They were parked under a grove of oak trees. She took a deep breath to remember how this felt. His taillights made the huge trunks red, and Annie's heart pounded. She was ready for this…whatever "this" was. When he'd finished parking, she distinctly heard "car wreck." She opened her eyes. His lips were closing in and, again, she distinctly heard "car wreck."

"Did you hear that?" she asked him. Looking at his lips, she kept her focus. "Did you hear someone say 'car wreck'?"

"Gee minee Annie, that's not what you talk about at a time like this."

She listened and heard nothing else. She was determined not to miss the moment but she was puzzled. He hadn't heard it. His lips touched hers. Had it been inside the vehicle, or just in her head? He put his arm around her shoulder. Was it a man's voice or a woman's? Definitely an adult.

"Car Wreck!" This time the voice was definite. She could not decipher if it was a man or a woman's voice but this time there was something different. This time there was a definite knowing that she had in every part of her being that someone was going to die and they were going to die in a car wreck.

"Someone's going to die," she told her date, who was just beginning to glow with anticipatory perspiration. Annie could not help but need to hear it in her own voice, " I know someone's going to die and it's going to be in a car wreck."

"Geez! That's not the kind of thing you say when you're trying to make out! If you want to go home just say so. You don't have to get all weird! Gees, that's sick. Just say you want to go home! You don't have to start talking about car wrecks and people dying! Just tell me you want to go home!"

With that he started the new truck and pulled out of the grove, onto the road, and took her directly home without another word, other than an occasional mumble about "That's sick."

The next morning, she arrived at school to find a wave of weeping flowing through the classrooms. A friendly classmate, in fact the one who had taken her to a prom, had been killed the night before. He had died instantly in a car wreck. She was stunned. Part of her wondered if she should call last night's date to tell him what had happened but part of her knew that these were not the kinds of things that most people would talk about. She was too sad and shaken to say, "I told you so."

This was only the beginning. Over the next six months, several deaths were preceded by her knowing, and by the end of the fourth death, she felt as though she was trapped in a wind tunnel. Was she responsible? Were her thoughts causing death?

It all became compounded. Things began to move when Annie walked into a room. Chairs would move, books would fall and she could feel the presence of someone else in the room when no one was there. Annie was afraid to go to sleep. She was afraid to enter a room if no one else was in it.

She began to notice circles under her eyes in the mirror, but she could not tell anyone. She had been to the university with her parents where they studied Ishi. They made him stay in a room while they studied him and nothing was even said about him being a dreamer.

She was so tired, and she was so confused. One of her friends had aspirin for headache. Her friend took aspirin every day. Annie never knew if she really had pain or if she just liked to hear herself say, "I need to take an aspirin, I have a headache."

Annie had never had a headache, but she thought what she felt now must be very close.

There were no medicines at home. Warm washcloths, hot soups, heated rocks, warm milk, massage, rest and being sung to sleep were the remedies she knew. Annie borrowed the bottle, and swallowed a handful. She returned the bottle to her friend and her friend quickly went to the nuns.

One of the Sisters came to her and said she thought it would be best if Annie would come in and lay down in the infirmary. Her parents would be there to pick her up, shortly. The gentle nun asked her what had happened and Annie, so relieved to be asked, told her everything.

Annie wept at the opportunity to tell another human being what she had been experiencing. About the voice that said "car wreck," about the moving furniture, about the other dreams and the other deaths, about the presence of others in the room that she had sensed. The nun told her not to worry; everything would be fine.

Annie's parents came to pick her up. She and her parents were asked to come into the Principal's office to have a short conference. She went in and sat, still confused.

The Mother Superior looked at all three. She gently stated that it seemed best for all involved for Annie to see a psychiatrist, and when the psychiatrist thought things were better, it would be good for Annie to come back to school.

Before she left the school, her favorite nun, Sister Jan, took her aside. Sister J. actually belonged to some international physicist association. She had come to this school, in the middle of nowhere, because she often had opinions that made the church nervous but she was so certain of her calling that they never kicked her out; they just kept moving her to places that were more and more remote.

"I have something to tell you, Annie. I do not know everything that is happening with you right now. But, there's something I want you to know. In physics, they say that no form of energy ever really dies; it is only transformed. When wood burns, it becomes carbon and gas. Everything is always becoming. So, if you hear people who have died, or if they were somehow impacting your environment, in physics we would have to say, 'We cannot say that is impossible.' Real science and real religion are so much warmer than many people think." She hugged Annie. Annie looked at her and said, "Thank you."

Her parents were silent on the ride home but occasionally patted her hand or stroked her hair. Annie fell into her bed as soon as they got home and slept.

The next day Annie was taken to see a fat bald man and he asked her many questions about sex. She had never had sex, but he wanted to know whether she wanted to have sex with boys, or with girls, or if she ever thought about it. When she looked at him, and looked at his eyes, it looked as if he was happy to have a job where he could say the word "sex" with great frequency. She had never had sex. She had just gone on her first unsupervised date, which fell very short from a date that would have sex in it, because of the voice that she had hear telling her about the car wreck. But, she thought that, maybe, it was not a good idea to share that with Sexman.

Her mother had taken her to the appointment. On the drive home her mother looked determined. She looked at Annie and said, "When I take my daughter to a psychiatrist because she is having dreams, I have been in this white world too long."

The next morning Annie was put on a Greyhound bus to stay with her Grandmother Mary.

Mary was waiting for Annie when her Aunt and Uncle delivered her to the wooden steps and the solid screen door. Annie was comforted by the smell of the dust and hay and wood and sage. When her Grandmother hugged her, she felt entirely safe. Grandma laughed with a sound that said, "Oh, here is my little one who is just like me. Everything will be all right. You are just right." She laughed softly while she rocked her granddaughter with both of them still standing on the wrinkled wooden porch. They were the same height and they rocked in unison with the wind and the cottonwood tree that shaded them.

Over the next several days old Indian women appeared from everywhere. They came in and sat and talked and told stories. Everyone knew why Annie had come. Mary would occasionally explain, sometimes in a whisper, sometimes in her own language that always sounded like a song, sometimes in a high-pitched voice that sounded like the sharp creaking of a pine tree fighting a strong wind, "Annie is here because she was getting in trouble for 'delusions'...that's what the white people call visions and she could have been kicked out of school because she told them." Even when Mary spoke in Shoshone, the English word 'delusions' stood out. Annie thought maybe there was not even such a word in Indian.

The women cautioned Annie about her *walk*. They warned her that, at times, when she was dreaming a lot, or when the dead were talking to her, or she was seeing visions, she would need to respect her own body. She would need especially to be well rested, to take hikes or go to the mountains to absorb all the beauty that was put around her to help her stay balanced. They told her that she could wash in a creek, or in the sink if she had to, to cleanse herself and to remember that she was just a messenger.

The elder women came when she was awake and they came when she was sleeping. Some came to her in her dreams, if they had not been able to travel, or if they were already on the other side. Some spoke in the daylight. They all stroked her hair, and, as they touched her, waking and sleeping, she began to fully feel that they were with her and she was becoming them.

Some of them told her that she would need to remember these things because there was such a thing as evil. There were people and beings on the other side that could seek to destroy or discourage her. She needed to be able to recognize them and protect herself. She learned never to eat food from someone who did not have a right heart toward her and not to accept anything that they offered her.

Some of the women who came to teach her were from different tribes. One woman told her to burn wild celery root when a new person came into the room. "If they're evil they will say 'what stinks'?" If it is a good person, they will say, "What is that that smells so good?"

Another very tall Indian woman told her that she should make a medicine pouch to wear around her neck and she should pray about what to put in it. Reminding her that there would definitely be times when she needed to protect herself, one old woman said, "Burn sage and pray", another said, "Burn cedar and pray" and still another said, "Burn sweet grass and pray." Mary told Annie, when she could see she was getting confused, "Just pray, then burn what your prayer tells you to burn. It is just something to remind the spirits that they have stepped into the physical world, and that's why it smells. It reminds them that it's time to go home, and the good ones will be happy to hear you pray."

There were so many times to pray. Pray when you gather herbs. Pray thanks for the herbs and thanks to the Creator for making them; pray to thank each healing plant that it would be willing to give its life to help someone heal. Pray healing for whoever would take any plant medicine, and pray for wisdom to knowing who should, or should not, use the medicine.

Pray especially when you prepare food. Pray for the people who eat it, that it would help them and cover them with good. That it would taste good and fill their souls and their stomachs. At times she felt her cynicism encroaching. Why in the world would the Spirits be so obsessed with food, eating and cooking and serving?

In Catholic school, Annie got the impression that their entire focus of the dead would be communing with God. Here, God, and food, and the dead, and the living were all intermingled as if they were all together for a family gathering. When she found herself beginning to be critical of the teaching, she remembered that she had somehow ended up in new terrain; she had certainly not been successful trying to plot her course alone. These women had the road map. Some had come across states to let her know how she could negotiate this new landscape.

Annie learned that she should pray about whether or not to tell someone when they were in her dream. She learned that her job, when she knew of some impending catastrophe, was to pray, both for the person who might die or be injured and for all of their family. She was especially to pray that everyone take the time to make amends.

She learned about the dead. She learned that they sometimes needed to be told that they were dead, especially if they died young or suddenly. She was told that some of the dead are stubborn, just like in life. With them, if they hang around too long, it might be necessary to be rude and hurt their feelings. With those beings she learned to shout at them and chastise them, she must say, "You don't belong here anymore. Go on! You are dead. You're not alive anymore and you're bothering people." She also learned that some people don't want to let the dead go.

Someone told Annie about her Great Grandmother and her husband. They fought until Great Grandma died. They both lived in a tee pee behind the house, and Great Grandpa knew exactly how to really push Great Grandma to her limits. She would holler at him and throw all his things out of the tee pee. He would hang around and, eventually, she would take him back in. No one could keep track of how many times she threw him out and how many times he moved back in. There were theories about how their relationship lasted so long. One was that he was the only man who was as stubborn as she was.

What almost went unmentioned was that Great-Grandpa was dead. None of the old women thought it was unusual that they were talking about a husband who had died in the woman's youth and was dead for nearly half of their marriage. What was uniformly admired was that they stayed together and fought, and loved, until the day she died.

The days, the brown faces, the long gray hair, short gray and black hair, all ran together. The instructions stopped being sounds and went into her heart. Soon she began to feel her feet. Then, she could very definitely feel the ground and the world was clear. Annie could feel her body, her shoulders, breasts, thighs, and back. Every part of her was sound and solid, and she could also feel that as she stood, those on the other side stood with her.

Annie learned not to be afraid. She was reminded that she had many more relatives who had already died, than she did relatives who were living. She was reminded that even if she did not know them, they knew her, and watched out for her.

Many relatives came with stories to strengthen her. It was as though they were each reminding her that these stories supported her.

Annie finally had a dream, which was not like a dream at all. It was more real than the itch that was left on her cheeks by the lye soap that her Grandma made. She dreamed the most fragrant dream she had ever smelled. Annie dreamed that she was lying in a thatched willow branch hut. The frame was covered with fresh, fragrant sagebrush, and there were old Indian women all around her. The eldest was burning sage. One by one they touched her as the oldest woman prayed and brushed her with the sleepy smoke.

In her dream, which felt more real than the waking world, Annie began to feel a powerful clarity. All of the women sang as she began to sit up. Then, one by one, the women left the hut, singing, each stepping into line, and singing, and walking out into the sagebrush; dancing, almost floating toward the lava mountain before them.

Annie knew when it was her turn and she stepped out onto the ground. The oldest Grandma was behind her still covering her with the clean smoke from the smoldering sage. Annie began to sing. One pure and beautiful song, a healing song, a power song, came to Annie as if all of her life, and all of her being, had been meant for this moment when she and this song would meet. She felt the ground and the sky in a way she never had before. As she walked with the women in the desert, singing, and she felt entirely sure of every note, every sound, and every step. As Annie sang, the song taught her and she knew fully in that moment, that in her own life she would feel incredible pain, and she would feel incredible joy. Annie sang, with all of her being, in celebration of both.

9

THE VISITOR

There was no question for Annie's family that love could endure beyond the grave. It was not rare that there were many ways that those who had died could check on their parents, or spouses, or children. It was also never questioned that Coyote had as much a part in the lives of those who were alive today, talking on telephones, as he had those who had already passed from this world who had known how to talk with the animals.

Annie remembered the morning that a woman in her thirties came over to Grandma Mary's house. It was still early. The men were in the fields, but the frost had not fully left the wooden planks outside the screen door that opened to Mary's house.

When the woman came in, she said hello in Shoshone. She frequently and easily flowed between Shoshone and English. The woman at first took care to be cordial, but shortly was moved to tears as she told about her evening with the Coyote.

Annie sat on the bed under the window that was covered with one of Mary's quilts. She tried to be invisible so she would not interrupt (and would not be asked to leave) the woman's account of Coyote's visit.

The woman sat across from Grandma Mary. Mary had comforted widows and orphans for nearly a hundred years and she knew exactly how to sit with this woman who had lost her father. The woman first covered formalities. Thank yous for pies at the funeral, thank yous for helping her to know what would help her father on his journey.

Eventually, there were tears as she recounted her night before coming to Mary.

As Annie sat completely still, Mary softly wiped the tears from the cheeks of the woman as she encouraged her to let her words have their life.

"Last night, very late, Arnie and I were in bed. It was still hot, so we had left the front door open, but we had the screen door locked. All the windows were opened and we could hear the frogs and the grasshoppers, and we could smell the cut alfalfa coming in the window. We were about to fall asleep, when we heard a coyote sing."

"At first, the song and the sweet alfalfa were helping us to fall asleep. Then Arnie stiffened, as we listened to the Coyote Song, and he asked, 'Why aren't the dogs barking?'"

"My whole body felt something strange about the quiet; it was different that the dogs were not barking. You know they always bark when they hear a Coyote. It is as though they are saying, 'We are not the same'… even though we know there are times when some of the male dogs are tempted by the Coyote women and we suddenly see coyote pups who are bigger than their cousins."

Mary sat as a layered lavender sunset came into view, open to the woman's story, not rushing, not judging, just staying. The woman continued. Annie made every effort not to move on the bed in spite of her increased interest.

"Arnie and I lay in the bed. The wind was coming in the bedroom and the Coyote kept singing; then we both knew that the dogs were giving him room for his song. We both lay on the bed and agreed that we did not know of this ever happening. We both, eventually, fell asleep and I think we woke at the same time; we heard a scratching on the screen door."

"Arnie moved so quickly, and he grabbed the shotgun standing behind the bedroom door. As he headed for the door, I knew I needed to get up and be there too."

"When we got to the front door, there was a Coyote with his hands on the screen, standing on his back legs looking at both of us through the mesh."

"I think Arnie was scared and he said, "I'm going to shoot him!""

"But, Mary" the woman whispered, "As Arnie lifted his gun to shoot the Coyote, I looked in the eyes of the Coyote and I shouted at Arnie not to shoot him. Mary, I told Arnie that I was pretty sure that it was my Dad coming to check on me. He was wanting me to know that he would watch me, and he was going now."

"Arnie has always been good to me, and when I looked at him, and he looked at the Coyote, he knew it was true."

"Arnie looked at the Coyote and said, 'Good-bye Dad.' Then, I looked at the Coyote, and I said, 'Good-bye Dad.'"

"Then, Coyote, with his paws on the screen looking in at both of us, I think he smiled...I really think he smiled. Then he dropped back to all fours and he ran out into the night. Our dogs never did bark at him."

The visiting woman seemed calmed after giving her story to Mary. She breathed deeply, as if she had come out of the water after a long swim and one tear came up from the water with her. As she looked in Mary's eyes, "You know," she spoke with a new peace, "the dogs never barked at Dad either."

Mary seemed not to move, but she handed the woman a piece of apricot pie. Then, in the sweet smell of the apricots, Mary began to tell her Coyote stories. The woman stayed, and cried, and laughed, and ate pie, and when she left, she was entirely glad that her father had come to tell her that he was ready to go. He just needed to stop and tell her, "Goodbye."

In Annie's tribe, the legend was that when you die you get to go up to the stars and dance among them. The really old people did not used to say "When I die" ...they would say, "When I go dancing." When Annie went to church they said she could live in a mansion. "In my father's house are many mansions." So it was dance with the stars or live in a mansion.

She imagined that being both white and Indian she would be able to pick. She wasn't sure which she would pick or if, in fact, she could do both.

Annie once had to choose between an invitation to a Victorian Tea and a Pow Wow. The decision was so tiring; she decided to do neither. Instead she went up to the mountain and gathered Mullein to dry for the fall and winter. When she came home, she had some Spearmint tea in a bone china cup that had soft lavender Petunias painted all around the cup and on the saucer. There was even a Petunia painted on the inside of the cup that looked at her when she lifted the warm cup to take a sip.

Often, as Annie grew, she could see no one else walking where she was. But, she knew that made it even more important that she walk with her feet planted firmly on the ground, like an Indian, not just on her toes, but firm footed, so that nothing could disturb her stance.

Past, present, and future did not mean what it, apparently, did for other people. When Annie talked with someone in the vegetable section at the market she could often feel it if they had lost a family member in the recent past. She had looked at people in the check-out line and seen their death. At times when she met someone new she could see that she would love them for a long time, that they would lay together, or they would travel together, or they had shared some grief in the past. She was remotely interested in supporting people who talked about a time continuum. She understood that as a reality.

The living and the dead were not so separate. Some people who walked as though they were living were much more connected to the land of the dead than the living. Some of the dead did not even know that they were no longer alive. Some people walked with grace solidly in the land of the living, with many of their dead relatives and lovers around them. That was always beautiful to feel.

Annie knew that much of her gift involved prayer; she would often pray for everyone in her family. She would pray for their health, safety, and purpose in their lives. She would pray that they would be blessed with appreciation for the simple and perfect things like good water, fish and venison, and above all, the love of family.

One day she was praying for her family. She always went by age, eldest to youngest, so that she wouldn't forget anyone. She was down to her brother Slim. She was opening her heart and her mind to pray for all good things for him when she got a reeling pain in the left side of her head. She was instantly dizzy and thought she would vomit.

She immediately reached for the phone. She could not sense what had happened but she was aware that the stabbing pain was Slim's. There was no answer.

Several times she dialed, frantically, finally deciding instead of wasting her energy on dialing she would pray for his safety; pray for the pain to leave both him and her. Soon she felt peace and the pain in her head subsided. She took a deep breath and dialed Slim again. He answered.

"Slim, this is Annie, are you all right?"

"Yeah, I'm all right. Why?"

She explained, "I was praying for you a little bit ago and I got a horrible pain in my head. I almost got sick it hurt so badly. Maybe I got mixed up and it was someone else."

"No, it was me. I was outside in the barn boxing with Arnold. I'm trying to get back into shape for firefighting so we've been trying to box a little bit every day. He just hit me with a good right cross. Well, actually he hit me so hard I got sick to my stomach and had to sit on a hay bale. I just came back in. It was me all right. But I'm fine."

She felt her body relax. "Slim?"

He answered, "Yeah."

"Could you guys switch to basketball?"

When Annie was a woman she met a beautiful man. She could feel his wounds, and feel his kindness. Some said he was handsome but, since she was so happy with how he felt, she did not really ever notice what he looked like. He was a hard worker and he helped her to grow.

She often dreamed for him. When he had business conversations on the phone, she could tell him if the man on the other end of the phone was honest. She could feel when he was in danger, or afraid, or flirting. She knew when he didn't make it home on time that he had stopped and talked with someone. It was not infrequent that she knew who he was visiting with. She felt him and she listened to the ancestors around him. That was just how it was.

One morning, before dawn, she woke from a dream that she knew she had to tell him. His pickup was already running outside. He had to leave early that morning so she jumped out of bed to tell him her dream. There was some danger in the dream and she felt some anxiety that he might be in too big a hurry to listen.

He was surprised to see her running in her nightgown in the dark toward him. He told her he didn't have time to hear about a dream, he was in a hurry. She nearly screamed at him about the dream. He stopped his pickup and looked her in the eye. "God! I wish you would stop dreaming for me. If I need to have a dream, I'll dream! I'm sick and tired of you dreaming for me and then expecting it to mean something to me." He started the pickup and backed up quickly, running over a chunk of firewood in his haste.

She stood outside and watched the tail lights fade. Then, she looked to the East and watched the sun beginning to outline the mountains with soft light. She felt her fear and her sadness, and she felt the pressure of *knowing* a danger that she could not share.

As she watched the sun coming up, standing on the cool dirt in her bare feet, she knew that she needed to pray. First, she prayed for the man. She prayed for his safety. She prayed that all of his ancestors would protect him and she prayed that the Creator would spare her more grief. She prayed that even if he could not hear the dream, he would see the danger.

Then, she prayed something she had never prayed. She prayed, first with sadness then with certainty, "I thank you that you have decided that I am strong enough to see the things I do. There are many times when I do not think I can hold the pain. I try to remember that you are not asking me to change the world. You are only asking me to pray. But this time, I have to tell you that I think you are asking me to do something that I am not strong enough to do. I don't think my dreams and my prayers are meant to make anyone angry. I cannot help but feel that I need to share the dreams that you give for this man. I will carry anything that you think I am strong enough to carry but, I need to ask if you are all right with it, that I have no more dreams or visions for that man. I have told every dream and every thing that I saw, but it is too hard for me to give something to someone who does not want to receive it."

"I am just your messenger, but I have to ask you, if you want to show him something, please, would you do it. I do not want to be asked to carry any more messages to him. So please do not send them to me. I ask to no longer feel what he is feeling and I ask not to know what he needs to know. I ask you to protect him today but please don't show me any more about his fate."

As the sun came up, Annie felt sad but she felt, somehow, lighter.

From that day it changed. She no longer felt him coming up the road. She could not feel his kind thoughts or his encounters. He was still a hard worker. He would still do anything to help her grow but she could only see him when they were in the same room together like a piece of flesh, like a deer hanging. Sometimes she could look and see that he had handsome features but there was nothing in her that could hear any part of him or anything about him. She knew that her prayer had been answered. Indeed, unlike all other beings in the world, she could not feel him. Somehow she was free, and so was he.

10

AꟅH BREAD

As Annie's Aunts got older, there were times that everyone gathered to try to learn, to try to feel, what it meant to be a part of this small ancient band.

One of the efforts involved the making of "ash bread." All the Elder Aunties gathered, many of the cousins, grandchildren, whoever was able, and there would be a feast and an introduction to one of the old ways.

Of course, the Eldest Auntie, now in her 90's, was the Mistress of Ceremonies, and did much of the directing. Elder Auntie was one of the old ones who had seen the change. As a young girl she had gone with her Grandma to the hills to gather seeds. She would gather, and be bored, and gather again as she heard the hum of her Grandma's prayers. "Creator, thank you for these seeds. Creator, thank you for this perfect day, and Creator, watch over this young girl who gets distracted from gathering seeds. Creator, watch over this girl whose heart is wondering, longing for something else, something more than gathering these seeds that will take care of all of her people. Creator, watch over this beautiful, stubborn girl."

Great Auntie had gathered seeds and roots with her Grandma and she knew what it was that the young one needed to learn. Great Auntie knew how to assign the tasks and she knew who was best suited for each task. As Annie did her assigned duties, she thought she heard her Auntie mumble something about "Creator, help this stubborn girl."

Annie looked across the sagebrush. She stood very still as she saw the Coyote standing on the horizon. She felt both vindicated and irritated as she looked at the Coyote when he trotted off, and she realized that he had been laughing.

Some had to dig a pit. Others gathered sage-brush branches, some younger ones, under Elder Auntie's instruction, stripped the branches so that they had nice, fragrant, twisty brown branches for the fire. One Uncle had been instructed to bring fine, clean creek sand. He unloaded big silver buckets from the back of his pickup truck and poured the sand from the big buckets into the pit that several of the nephews had dug. Great Auntie instructed him to remember to save a couple buckets of sand. The Elder Auntie directed that the sand already in the pit be packed smooth. She instructed that the small branches be broken into pieces and directed that they be placed in the pit when it was ready. Beautiful, strong river rocks were placed to carefully encircle the pit.

While Elder Auntie choreographed the pit project, Auntie Millie directed the mixing of fry-bread dough. A circle of nieces was under her direction as several big bowls of fry-bread dough were made. The whole time, she clarified the names of the different roots that would have originally been used to make the bread dough. She stated that it was important to know that the original ash-bread was much better than this "diabetes bread." Auntie Millie then gave a free lecture on the theory that the introduction of white flour and lard into the Indian communities was killing Indian people because their bodies could not easily metabolize these white foods. She lectured on restricting intake of these two "Indian killers."

A line of young women made platefuls of bread patties and little girls had clumps of dough to shape into little balls. One of the little nephews asked for a piece of dough to work with and immediately turned it into a baseball, which stuck to a willow tree trunk as soon as he threw it. The order was given that he was to get no more dough as one of his Uncles could be heard hollering, "Good throw!!!"

When everything was ready, Great Auntie instructed that the fire be lit. The sage crackled and made the most wonderful smell. Everyone talked more quietly and there was the feeling of an efficient military unit that had just completed a mission and was waiting for the next.

When the fire burned down, the Elder Aunt took her long walking stick and began to dig into the hot, clean, gray ashes. She instructed one of the girls to begin to lay the round, flattened dough patties on the ash, one by one. One of Elder Auntie's "little sisters" (in her 70's) came rushing over to the pit with a bread-sized piece of tin foil. Her fry-bread was wrapped in foil!

As she dropped her foil-wrapped bread into the pit, her big sister chided her, "Hey! That's not how the Old Indians do it!"

Her little sister, who had beautiful wrinkles that were always smiling, grinned at her "big sister" and said, "When I'm an 'Old Indian', I'll do it the old way! For now, I just don't want ashes on my bread!"

Muffled giggles rippled through the family as the Elder Auntie began to cover all the bread with the ash that she had moved aside. They could not imagine what it must be like to talk to the Elder Auntie that way, and if anyone else didn't want ashes on their bread, they certainly didn't say so. When the bread was covered with ash, Great Auntie instructed that the ashes be covered with the remaining sand, and the dirt surrounding the pit was carefully placed over the sand.

As they watched the nephews covering the pit, a little red Camaro pulled up, and a long, young Indian man stepped out of the car. A string of like-aged young women looked at the ground and slid glances toward him as he slowly walked toward the Elder Aunt. Everyone pretended to give him privacy but fully listened to everything he said.

He was working on a Master's Degree in Anthropology and explained that he had a theory about passive farming techniques having been used by Nomadic people, which the Shoshone were. He was also Shoshone but from a band some miles away. Someone had advised him that the Elder Auntie would be able to help him identify a number of edible roots, which he had gathered. He had them in the car, if she would be willing to look at them.

Great Auntie told him she would and she and her sisters lined their chairs together to review the roots. As he took each one out of the bag, there would be discussion among the four sisters and their sister-in-law. Great Auntie would announce the name in Shoshone and then she would nibble the root. Occasionally, one of her sisters would contest her verdict and ask to taste the root for confirmation. The young man took notes and looked alternately elated and concerned.

At the end of the review, the young man had pages of information and an empty bag. The timing was perfect. At the last swallow, the Great Auntie said it was time to uncover the ash bread.

Several of the nieces looked at Great Auntie imploringly. She noticed and invited the tall young man to stay. He declined and thanked her, respectfully, for all the information she had given him.

One of the nieces followed him to his car. "I hope you got what you needed."

"Oh," he said, "I got more information than I had thought I would be able to find."

She looked at him, puzzled, "Then why do you look worried?"

"Well," he said quietly, "Great Auntie just ate the exhibits for my thesis. I'm just hoping that the pictures I took of the roots turn out."

They had shared a secret, and they both laughed, and knew that this would not be the last time they would see each other.

The dirt, and sand, and the ashes were taken out of the pit. The bread was put on plates and the clean ash was dusted off. All of the relatives ate the bread that had been cooked in their ancestor's oven.

11

MICHAEL

Annie had one beautiful child, a son. His eyes were the shape of almonds, and his hair had the look and feel of blue-black river rocks, reflecting the sun in a stream of tickling cold, fresh creek water. His little lips were as soft as new spring moss and his laugh carried like a waterfall from his heart into the hearts around him. He was a child who tried out his new umbrella in the shower when it did not rain. He sympathized with Dracula because he didn't have many friends. He asked the man who raised him, when they were waiting out a storm while fishing, "Do worms yawn?"

He wondered, "If God is everywhere, why don't we bump into him once in a while?"

He had his own way of forming conclusions: "Mom, do you know how I know that God hears my prayers? He has never once said, 'Huh'?"

Annie had known when he was born that she needed to name him for an angel. And her heart hurt when she named her beautiful son Michael.

There were times that she knew that he was like her, like her Grandmother. She knew that it was not easy.

As Michael grew, Annie really worked hard. She took care of her son, paid much of her money to childcare so that the sitter would always be there, so she could keep her job, and her son.

Annie worked with people all day. She counseled, encouraged, transported, laughed, scolded, and prayed. One evening after supervising a college recruitment field trip her feet hurt, and her eyes stung with tired. She held her toddler son as she went to get the eggs, celery, and the milk and grapes that she knew she had left in the fridge. It wasn't a lot but it was good nutrition.

Annie opened the fridge. There, on the top rack was one giant venison leg. Someone had come in while she was gone, opened the fridge, and left a huge burgundy deer leg in the fridge. She and Michael both laughed with surprise.

Annie put Michael down. They told hunting stories while she pulled the leg out and cut through the fascia that looked like satin and always got stuck between her teeth.

She cubed several pieces, rolled them in flour with a little salt, black pepper, and a touch of cayenne. Out came the wrought iron skillet, and Crisco. Annie heated the grease that always reminded her of the glue paste they had at school when she was little. When the grease was hot, she put in the floured meat, and they heard the "hissssss." Annie and Michael both clapped their hands and the little one said, "YAYYYY!"

They sat at the table and ate. Michael asked, "Who brought the deer meat, Mom?" Annie said, "Maybe it was an angel."

And she thought of all the angels she knew. She knew the brown angel with the smile wrinkles who was a licensed mechanic until he went deaf. He fixed her car to keep her on the road for college. He knew that she secretly thought he was beautiful.

She thought of the brown angel who married her sister. He could skin a deer in 60 seconds by cutting the hide inside the legs, making one quick slit down the deer's belly, and pulling the skin off like one tight coat.

Annie thought of the brown angel who watched her, but partied too much. He knew that she had picked a different path, and he loved her for it.

She thought of the brown angel who had fathered her son and had not been good to her. She knew, now, that she might not forget that.

She thought of the brown angels that she had counseled who needed hope; some slept on mattresses or in the car if the house was too noisy. After she and Michael ate and talked, she washed the dishes, washed the little one, tucked him in, and she went to bed.

As she lay in bed, she found herself still thinking, all the way into her dreams, about all the brown angels who could have put the deer meat in the fridge.

12

SEEING

Once Annie and Michael had taken one of Michael's friends for an excursion. They walked, with sandwiches, through a park and around a large pond on a warm day with a blue sky uninterrupted by clouds. His friend, in days past, would have been called his cousin.

In Annie's tribe, close women became like sisters and their children were like cousins.

Vernon's mother was like a sister to Annie. Their Grandmothers had been very much alike. Both of their Grandmothers had known ways of dreaming and healing, and *walking*, which were only told in whispers now. For whatever reason, Annie and Vernon's mother had difficulty speaking on the telephone to each other. Wherever these "sisters" were, if they attempted phone conversation, tremendous static eventually interrupted. No matter how many places they called each other from, no matter how many conversations each had successfully had earlier in the day, the static would build until they could no longer hear each other clearly. Eventually they would say, "Our Grandmas are interfering. I'll talk with you later."

Vernon was familiar with visions and dreams. As they walked through the park and around the pond, Michael stopped sharply. "Did you see that guy?"

Annie looked at her son, only 11, and in his brown almond eyes she could immediately see the clarity that comes with seeing two worlds.

She asked him very calmly, "What did you see?"

He looked a little frantic, but definite. "That blonde guy…the one who just got out of the water? Did you guys see him?"

There was a different feeling to Michael's question and Annie knew how it felt when one first stepped into the other side. She was so grateful that it was Vernon who was with them.

"Let's go over to where you saw the man, okay?" she asked her son.

They walked to the edge of the pond where Michael had been looking. Annie asked him, "Where did you see him?"

The pond was small, circular, manmade, and surrounded with golden sand. Michael pointed, "I saw him right here." He was definite about where he'd seen him.

Annie encouraged the boys to walk with her to the edge of the pond where Michael had pointed. She prayed and then she began to talk to the boys. "You both had Great Grandmas who dreamed and saw visions, and knew things that not everyone knew. In both of your families, this is something that is very normal."

"Now this is where you saw a blonde man get out of the pond?" Michael nodded confirmation. Then, Annie calmly put her hand on her son's shoulder and pointed to the ground, "There is not water here. You can see that the sand is dry and we would be able to see some water where the man stood when he got out. If you look behind us, you can see the tracks that each one of us made in the sand. Mine are a little deeper than yours because I am a little bigger, but you can see that the man left no tracks. Also, I want you to look. We can see quite a ways in every direction. If someone had just gotten out of the pond, we would see him on the road or we would see him over on the flat. He just got out and we cannot see him."

"I just saw him!" Michael said, a growing stress in his voice.

Annie looked at him and looked at Vernon and said, "I know you saw him. But, the man you saw is not a live person. You should not be nervous about it. You saw a spirit. You definitely saw him. You know what he looks like. There is a reason that you saw him and there is a reason that it is just the three of us."

"You have to know that you have nothing to do with this. You just saw this so that we could pray. Now, we don't know who the man is, or what has happened, but we do know that he and his family need prayer, so that's what we all will do right now."

She was aware of their pre-adolescent sensitivities so Annie reminded them that they could not see anyone and she asked them to both pray with her.

"For whoever it is that Michael saw, and for his family, we pray. We thank you for having us come along to this place at the right time. We know that we have no power over what is meant to be but we ask that everyone be comforted in whatever their situation might be. Thank you that Vernon and Michael both come from people who have heard the many kinds of things that you wanted to be heard. Please help us to always remember to do our part if something like this comes up. Help us to remember to pray."

As Annie opened her eyes from their prayer, she was compelled to look into the pines across from the pond. She found herself squinting, trying to see something faintly, that she had seen clearly with her eyes closed, and there it was. Annie took a deep breath as she watched the Coyote tail disappear into the woods.

With that, she encouraged the boys to enjoy the day. She gently told them if they felt bad or concerned, they should pray again, for the man and his family.

When she took Vernon home, she and Vernon's mother had a long talk. They were glad that their boys had both been introduced to the other world. But they both also felt a burden for the man by the pond.

The next morning Annie woke up to the telephone ringing. It was her friend, Vernon's mother. "Did you get the newspaper yet?"

Annie mumbled, "No, Why?"

Vernon's mother paused and then told Annie, "A man drowned at the pond where Michael saw him yesterday."

Annie worried for Michael. She knew how difficult it could be to "know" things outside of an Indian community. "Seeing" things, as Michael had, as she did, as her Grandmother had, had little place in dominant society. Non-Indians (as they called them) were mainly trying to "*become* someone," so they often did not like to have someone see them as they were. They were "self made," and some did not like to think they had ancestors who were advocates or participants in their lives. So many of their chosen realities had to do with self..."self made, self directed, self sufficient, self motivated. Annie thought perhaps so much "self" was what came from a people looking in mirrors for thousands of years. For indigenous people, their only mirror was the reflection of the water in a lake or pond. The sky, the clouds, the birds, other laughing faces, the trees, all accompanied the reflection of one's own small face.

If Annie had a dream outside of the Indian community, and dreamed that someone was afraid, the intention of the dream was so they would not feel alone. But, dreaming did not work easily on the outside. Annie, early on, would obey the ancestors. If they told her in a dream, or while she was awake, that someone was afraid, she would tell that person about her dream. "They" (non-Indians) often did not have permission to call upon their ancestors. They did not have permission to be afraid of being alone, and they certainly did not have permission to listen to a young woman they did not know, bringing them a dream.

Soon she found that was not comfortable for her or for them. Annie would do as she was taught. She would take the dream to the person it was sent for. Outside of her community, most often people thought she was crazy. The non-Indians had many ways of running from their own dreams; they certainly could not stand with Annie and hers. Annie faced the knowing that they might turn from Michael, too.

13

HIGHER ED

The Adult Indian Education Program where Annie worked reminded her daily about the interconnectedness among American Indians, or Native Americans, as they called themselves.

Annie did student recruiting, counseling, and tutoring, trying to give access to education to Native American students who had been discouraged by mainstream instruction. She went to the homes at the end of dirt roads, into big, soft, leather-brown dirt lots that sometimes seemed to be full of more cars than the homes had people. She knew some of the cars ran and some were for parts. Some had just come to stay.

Annie did Community Outreach. She would sit on the porch steps with elders and explain what they were trying to do at the Indian Education Center for Indian students.

On her way down one dirt road, leading to one of the houses, she met an old woman picking blackberries on the road. Her hair was neatly combed, braided, and wrapped into a tight bun that clung to the back of her head. Both sides of her face had been splashed with laugh lines. The old woman was one of the elders who always had so many children in her care; most of the young people didn't know, anymore, which ones where her relations and which were strays. But she loved them all.

Annie stopped her car and walked through the knee-high wild wheat grass to the fence line where the old woman was picking.

The woman smiled when she saw Annie walking over to talk with her. Annie smiled back as her own hands began to automatically find the biggest, soft blackberries to put into the woman's cut-open milk carton.

The old woman knew who Annie was and she looked at her with a warm mischievous glow. The woman said, "I know you're that girl who's talking to people about Higher Ed, aren't you?"

Annie continued to pick. "Yes I am."

The woman stopped picking, looked at Annie, and she smiled. Then she began to giggle. "Higher Ed! Higher Ed! Everyone always says it will help all these Indian kids. I wish *someone* would hurry up and hire Ed, whoever he is, and then maybe these kids wouldn't have such a hard time in school!"

Annie and the woman both laughed, and when the carton was full, Annie said her goodbyes. The next day several new students came in; they said that the old woman told them they had to come.

Mainstream education at the college level was awkward for many of the Indian students. There were times when even Annie's bicultural exposure did not prepare her for the sting of dominant society academic concepts.

Annie remembered when her sister took Cultural Anthropology in College and was introduced to the term "North American Aboriginal People." Annie had found her sister crying in the bathroom after class. "They called us Aborigines! Can you believe that?" Her sister mumbled between blowing her nose, "You and your mother are Abos!" She laughed with her sister and they made it through their classes, even when they had to sit through courses in which they were lectured on "Social Stratification." They looked for a long time when they studied together and found that there was an actual graphic to show that a brown nurse was not as high on the ladder as a white one. A white father, married to a brown woman, was not as high on the ladder as a white man married to a white woman. However, a white man married to an uneducated white woman was really standing on the same step as a white man married to an educated brown woman. It was very complicated and varied from country to country, group to group.

There were numbers, bar graphs, and tests to make sure that you knew that this was someone's truth. Here, it was the only truth that counted.

The white students seemed to stand alone. Some thought it was strange that Annie, her sister, her mother, and other Indian students would feel the need to be with each other. They thought it was curious that they spoke so much of family. Some of them seemed to pretend that they had no family. Some maybe did not know that they had family that had come before them. Something about it was a puzzle for Annie. They identified themselves as "self made." Many did not think they had ancestors who were advocates or participants in their lives. Annie only knew that something always felt off balance to her when she was with these people who believed the world started with them.

14

OLD MAN JOHNSON

The difference between the Adult Indian Education Project and the mainstream college was most glaring in the case of Old Man Johnson.

Old Man Johnson was a Northwest Coastal Indian who had lived for more than 100 years. He had seen the many changes that any centenarian had experienced and he had grown up nearly one hundred years ago, with his own Grandfather who connected him to a time when many families carved their own canoes. He was related to the cedar trees and to the Raven.

Old Man Johnson came from generations of storytellers and song carriers. He taught traditional dances to young students with his skinny, bird-bone arms flapping slowly like a raven in flight. Students of every age would sweat as they struggled to find that place of grace that he seemed to always be standing alone in.

Old Man Johnson had come south for the winter to visit one of his granddaughters, and he was willing to come to the Indian Education Center to do a presentation for the Native American History class. The class was from 3pm to 5pm every Tuesday and Thursday. The word went out that Old Man Johnson had said he would come.

The day Old Man Johnson came, the smell of food permeated the Center building. His granddaughter pulled up in her light blue Ford pick-up. Two young men were instantly there to help Old Man Johnson out of the truck. He moved like a mountain goat, and the young men just walked with him, joking and introducing themselves. By the time they arrived at the Center conference room, the old man had told each of the boys stories he had heard about their Grandfathers, and in some of the stories he had been a participant.

Old Man Johnson was given a chair and a glass of water, and the students in different shades of brown and cream encircled him. With some in chairs, some on the floor, he had a willing and attentive audience. Everyone stood as Old Man Johnson began to pray. Some nodded, some smiled, and all of the room prayed to the Creator to ask for blessing on all that he would say, and the way that they would hear, as they all came together in this place. After he prayed, everyone got comfortable as he began to tell and sing his stories, the stories of old time, and the stories of the time when Mother Earth was happy and loved.

As the stories continued, the circle began to grow. Some left to pick their children up from day care. Some returned with little faces in tow, some clean, some dusty. One who had been crying when her nap was interrupted and had little silver snail tracks on her cheeks that started at her nostrils.

Old Man Johnson told stories and sang, and stopped occasionally to nibble on something people from the community brought to thank and support his spirit and all of his relatives. One woman brought an oil-spotted brown grocery sack full of smoked salmon. She told the old man that she knew his people liked this kind of food because her Mother's Aunt was from a Northwest Coastal Tribe. She had always loved smoked salmon since she was a little girl. She and her family would go up north to visit her Auntie and she had learned to make it as a young woman.

Old Man Johnson said, "Thank you, girl." The young people chuckled because the "girl" was in her 70's.

The "Indian telegraph" was in good form. Young and old, all tribes, began to gather around the gifted storyteller. He talked and sang, and the faces in the room, and the ancestors in the room, laughed and cried. They all remembered until all of the little children were sleeping and dreaming to the hum of his song, the beat of his hand drum, and the touch of his stories stroking the cheeks of their sleeping faces.

When Old Man Johnson's niece could no longer keep her eyelids open, she said her Uncle needed his rest. The night wrapped his arms around the children, the young people, and the elders who had come.

They drove home, with their ancestors and Old Man Johnson still singing in their ears.

Old Man Johnson was going to be staying with his niece for several weeks. Annie was behind in her Native American Studies class on the Mainstream campus. She had needed to go to several funerals in the Indian community at the time that her classes were held, so she could not attend the lectures that had been given at the same time.

Everything in the Mainstream College was broken into points. There were points for tests, points for essays, points for attending and, in this class, if someone was low on points, there were extra credit options.

Annie had been looking at the options at the same time Old Man Johnson was in town. She noticed on the list one of the "extra credit" options was: Option 5. Arrange for a relevant guest speaker to present to the Native American Studies class.

Annie went to talk to Old Man Johnson's niece. She explained the whole story, why she had missed the classes (she had, of course, seen Old Man Johnson's niece at each of the funerals) and she explained to her about the number five extra-credit option. Annie knew that Old Man Johnson was a famous speaker and had even flown to Europe to talk to different groups. His dancers had even danced in Washington D.C. a couple times.

Old Man Johnson's niece got up from the kitchen table. She went outside where Old Man Johnson was sitting under an oak tree feeling the warmth of his walking stick as he gently stroked the stomach of the earth and her soft green hairs with the end of the wooden walking stick. He had carried the walking stick since his eighties when a large "Widow Maker" had nearly destroyed his leg. He had been helping a friend cut logs. Some had been very critical of the friend for taking such an old man into the woods. The "Widow Makers" were large dead branches which, normally, just fell to the forest floor when the wind blew or they just became tired of hanging onto life. No one knew when they would fall and anyone but Old Man Johnson would probably have been killed. He had danced all of his life and he heard the death song of the Widow Maker as she fell from the Redwood tree. He did a side-hop, Raven dance step that allowed him to avoid having his head directly crushed by the death dance of the Widow Maker.

Despite the criticism about how Old Man Johnson's friend had taken him into the woods, he and his friend both found the incident food for a powerful story. Each of the men was gifted in story telling. There had always been a quiet debate about whose version of the story was the most entertaining. The common thread in the story was that they were both very pleased that the Creator had opted not to have the Widow Maker fall on "O" (that was the name of Old Man Johnson's friend). It was the name that he had been given when he was a boy and a name that stuck with him into adulthood for obvious reasons. "O" was close to 6 feet tall and when one saw Old Man Johnson's friend walking toward them on the horizon, it looked exactly like the letter "O" was rolling your way.

Annie sat at the kitchen table and watched Old Man Johnson and his niece from the kitchen window. She knew that Old Man Johnson's niece would be telling him about her tribe and about her Grandpa who had gone to Carlisle, too.

Annie smiled as Old Man Johnson turned to look up at her in the window and he lifted his walking stick in greeting and nodded his head. Old Man Johnson was willing to come to the Native American Studies class at the Mainstream College.

Old Man Johnson's niece left him sitting under the oak tree so he could continue his courtship with the earth. She headed back into the house to let Annie know how much longer he would be staying with her so Annie would have some idea what to arrange in terms of dates.

Annie met with the instructor of Native American Studies. The class was held on Tuesdays and Thursdays. Tuesdays, the class was one-hour long and the Thursday class was two-hours long.

The instructor had many questions about Old Man Johnson. His biggest concern was, "Can the old man stay on track? If he's over a hundred, can he stay on track?"

Annie felt embarrassed because she was not really sure what that meant. She did not really know what "track" the instructor was talking about, and she felt confused as she repeated what she knew to be his greatest credential, "He is more than 100 years old."

"Okay," the instructor said, "I'll take a chance, but let's schedule him for the one hour next Tuesday in case he has a hard time staying on track. If we book him for Thursday two hours might be too long for him and the class, if he rambles."

Annie contacted Old Man Johnson's niece. She did not mention the questions about his staying on track because, although she did not entirely understand it, she was embarrassed for her teacher that he had asked.

On the day Old Man Johnson came to class he came wearing neat jeans, a wrangler plaid shirt, and a Plains Indian beaded vest. The vest was covered with white beads and had two horses beaded on the front. The horses were facing each other, one on each side of the front of the vest. The back had a beautiful geometric design in red, white and blue.

Old Man Johnson started with a prayer song. As he sang, some of the students sat in perfect stillness, some wrestled their note pads to prepare to take notes, some were drawn by their own life dramas to struggling to stay in their chairs, in this class, and college in general.

After singing the prayer song, Old Man Johnson began to pray. "Grandfather, thank you for bringin' me to this place. Thank you for askin' me to talk to these young people, that they would know about what happened on this land, and that they would know about the truth, that they would know about you and the way you take care of us. Grandfather, thank you for listenin' to me, as I asked you what I should say, and I thank you for making my words clear, and my heart strong. Grandfather, I'll say what you tell me an' I'll try not to let my words get in the way of what you would want these young ones to hear."

"Grandfather, you had me walk on this earth, so far, more than a hundred years and I wanna tell you that I am ready to walk on and leave this earth today if you are ready for me. Sometimes I think I been on this earth so long. Sometimes I wonder if you forgot about me. But I know, Creator, you know I am the one who was called Little Jim by my Mother and Father so long ago, when I first came here. I know you did not forget me but I just want to say I am ready to walk away from this earth whenever you are ready for me. I don't need nothin' fancy. I'm trying to live this life in a good way so I would come to you with clean hands and a clean heart. I'm ready, Grandfather, if you would ask me to come today.

"Grandfather, I come with the words you give me. I won't say more and I won't say less. I ask you to help me speak in a good way so these young people would know about you and Mother Earth and how you both take care of us. Help me, Grandfather. Help me to tell about the things that you and me talked about before I came here today. Thank you, Grandfather. Thank you for helping me in all that I have done as I have been walkin' here on this earth for more than one hundred years. If you are done with me, I am ready to come to you in a good way. This is Little Jim, Grandfather, sometimes known after all this time on Mother Earth, as Old Man Johnson."

Much of the room was quiet, some of the classroom was restless; one woman in her 50's made the sign of the cross in her seat when Old Man Johnson finished.

Old Man Johnson looked at his hands for a moment and then he began to talk. Occasionally he looked up at the faces in the classroom. "I'm gonna talk for a little while. You can listen if you want to. I'm not going to answer questions because I have prayed and I will say what the Creator has asked me to say. I'm not talking about anything else because I'm only gonna talk about what I know. I don't know anything more than what I'm gonna tell you."

He began to talk and tell stories. There was shifting in the seats. A couple of young white men looked at each other, and one mouthed, "Whaaat?"

Old Man Johnson talked about his tribe, changes he had seen, things he had learned, and he talked about the vest he wore. He told about how the vest had belonged to a friend of his who was a Plains Indian. He talked about how he and this friend had been friends for 70 years. He talked about how his friend had this vest, which had been made many years ago.

When his friend died, he came to him in a dream and he told him, "Johnson, you wear my vest. Now, I'm gone. My vest wants to be worn and it needs to be worn by someone who will be able to take it to different places because that is how it has been for the life of this vest so far. I am telling you now (his friend said in the dream) because I am dead and I want you to wear my vest."

So, Old Man Johnson explained to the class. He found out that his friend had died, and when he went to the funeral in the Great Basin Country, his friend's wife brought out the vest and told him that her husband had wanted him to have it. He explained that even though he was a North West Coastal Indian from a particular tribe. He wore this Plains vest to honor his friend, because travel and new faces were what the vest was used to.

Before the hour was up, the instructor came to the front of the class and interrupted Old Man Johnson's story, and said, "Are there any questions?"

Annie's cheeks burned with embarrassment, and Old Man Johnson, and his many years on the earth, quietly walked out of the room.

Annie and her sisters were not the only Native American students who were sometimes puzzled by the academic world and the people around them on campus. Once the three sisters were sitting in the cafeteria. One of the male Indian students, whom they had all adopted, came over looking rather pressured.

As he sat at the table, one of the sisters gave him an opening. "What's happening, Leonard, are you getting ready for a big test?" They each inquired in some way to let him know that he could say something about his pressures if he wanted to. Leonard was not a young student but he had decided, in his 30's, to take advantage of his veteran's benefits before it was too late. He had mainly lived in the mountains and had a huge extended family. He was big but he was clean and neat (when ragged was in fashion) and his hair was always braided smoothly. He once had a beautiful woman, when he was a very young man, but she left him for a white man. He had really not had a serious girlfriend since that time. Everyone knew sometimes he visited the gal who lived in the little cabin by the river. She was kind enough to keep every man warm who needed it, but that didn't really count as a girlfriend. The three sisters looked out for him because they had four younger brothers and they knew that no matter how big Leonard looked, he was little because he was still hurt.

Leonard looked down at his binder and began to lightly scratch the cover with his thumbnail. "Well, I guess I *am* about to be tested." Leonard still could not make himself look up.

"What is it, Leonard? We can help you study! You're not thinking about dropping out are you?"

Leonard took a deep breath and shyly glanced at the girls sitting like three little winter birds on a branch. "Well, here's the thing…there's a white lady who wants me to go out with her. I don't know if she wants to go out with *me* or if she's looking for some kind of 'Mystic Warrior' experience."

The three sisters looked at each other and Leonard, and Leonard began to laugh. They all laughed but they could still see that Leonard was actually concerned about it so they began to inquire about the woman. Had they met in a class? What class was it? What did she look like? How old was she?

As Leonard subjected himself to the third degree, they discovered that the woman was 50, close to 20 years his senior!

"My God, Leonard! 50! She's probably wondering if you're just interested in her because you have a thing for *old women*!"

They all laughed together and, with that, Leonard seemed to regain his composure and he got up from the cafeteria table. "Do any of you jealous women want a soda?"

Dominant society education was so lonely. There was little story telling. There was almost no laughter. Everything the book said was the truth. But Annie, and all of her family who had ever gone to school knew there were many more truths, truths not written in the books.

One day, in a U.S. history class, she overheard two young women talking about their family histories after a lecture on the Westward Movement. One of the young women said, "My family was one of the second waves to come to this country after the Mayflower." The other young woman said, "My family has been here since 1776 and I had a distant relative who was involved in drafting the Declaration of Independence."

The next time Annie saw her Grandmother she asked, "How long have we been here, Grandma?"

Her Grandma was sitting at the table, covered with the flowers of one of the aprons that she usually wore and she was snapping green beans. Her hands would quickly break off the ends, stripping the string out of the crack before she broke the bright emerald beans in half. Grandma laughed quietly. "Why do you ask?" She encircled a tremendous pile of green beans with her beautiful wrinkled hands and plopped them in front of Annie.

Annie began to join her Grandma in the snapping song the beans made. "Well, I just heard some people at college talking about when their families came here. I know when my Dad's people came but I don't know how long we've been here."

Grandma looked far away and she said, "Well, one of your cousins came back from college and said, "We've been here for 10,000 years." Another one of your cousins went to a different college, and when he came back he said, "Grandma, we've been here for 50,000 years."

Grandma continued to break the beans. It was as though her hands worked on their own. Annie felt clumsy to notice that this old women broke beans at five times the speed she was able to make her own young hands go. Grandma said, "I only know that all our ancestors and all our stories are here. If the animals could still talk, they would probably be able to answer your question."

Then Grandma laughed the laugh that was quiet but filled every corner of the room with fun. "Maybe the animals still talk but no one is listening."

For many years, of all the things that Grandma had told her, that was one of the things she wondered about the most. Could the animals still talk?

Annie tried to help the students in the Adult Indian Education Program where she worked. She tried to help herself, so that she could help her son. But the coldness of the Mainstream College, where she took courses, was exhausting. She found the energy to continue her studies when she laughed with her sisters and Mother and brothers, and Michael, and her friends.

She found energy when she walked on a dirt road, or camped on the weekend and woke to the smell of dust and water, cedars and pines, and the sound of the water playfully stroking the round breasts of the rocks.

Annie loved cooking firm fresh trout over the campfire. She always enjoyed the sweet smell of corn as she pulled back the husks, cleaned out the silk, and pulled the husk back over the corn before placing the corn beside the coals (leaving them just long enough to make the sweet corn warm and roasty tasting).

She felt strong when she lay on her back and watched the trees reach for the wind. She felt sure of herself when there was no building in sight and she could feel everything around her and she could hear the earth say, "You are home." She felt a sense of completion when she would turn to her son, lying on the ground, and tell him, before he went to sleep under the moon, "You are home."

One sleepy night she remembered looking up and seeing two cedars with their arms reaching out for each other, laced, and moving together rhythmically against the blue-black sky. Surrounded by stars (all the ancestors who had come before), they appeared to be doing the Two-Step that couples dance at the Pow Wows (some tribes call it the Rabbit Dance). Men and women with arms laced, couples hand-in-hand, glide in procession to the beat of the Pow Wow drum. When they dance, there often seems to be no time when they are earthbound. They are doing the dance of a man and a woman. Their arms move smoothly like the rhythm of the bobbing cedars. As Annie watched the cedars doing the Rabbit Dance, she could feel herself being held by sleep. She smiled as the rhythm of the wind played the drumbeat, as she and sleep joined the cedars in the dance.

Often people in the Indian community were so much more connected than Annie experienced in dominant society. As years passed Annie recognized that what they shared, which few people in the United States did, was place. They had been in this place for so long. Some tribes said they were created here, others say they were placed by the Creator, but for all of them there was someone for whom this land, this country, was a sacred place. Their songs, whether remembered in the mind or the soul, and their stories, were connected to this place.

Annie once heard two Jewish women, her own age, talk about which concentration camps their parents had survived. She recognized that what people in the Native community also shared was experience.

However, because of the story telling, the experience was collective, not individualized. A story was told for each person but more for the group. The story was told by the ancestors, long dead, and the intention was that it would be told to the children yet to come. The story was why so many in the family did not have clocks in the house and many did not own wristwatches. Clocks could be misleading; *story* told the time more accurately. The present was only the second hand.

15

AUNTIE BEAUTIFUL

Annie remembered an old Miwok woman asking her who her family was (by that she meant on her Indian side). Annie spoke her Mother's maiden name and the old woman looked at her with a grateful smile that somehow seemed out of place.

"Your Aunt saved my life," the round brown woman said as she pointed at her for emphasis. "She saved my life."

Annie knew not to interrupt while the old woman collected the thoughts and pictures and tastes that made that statement true for her.

"When I was a young girl, I got taken to boarding school. I went all the way from our field, all the way down to Riverside Indian Boarding School. I'm sure you've heard of it because your Auntie went there when she was younger. Then she ended up working there. They had some Indian students who stayed and worked at boarding school when they were done with their education because it was too hard on everyone when the children were all by themselves. They found out they needed to have some grown-ups around who were Indian. I came to the school in Riverside clear from Greenville, California."

"We had classes, and there was a place in the back of the room where we hung our coats. I thought I would die from missing my family."

"I was just a little girl. I had lots of brothers and sisters and Aunts and Uncles, cousins, and my Grandma, and my mom and dad. Everyone was fine, and we laughed a lot. Sometimes my brothers were naughty, but there was always someone around. You couldn't hide anything. Even though all kids want to get away with something, you couldn't because there was always someone around. If we tried to get away with something, when you got caught, everyone would laugh. We laughed a lot."

"When I came to boarding school, I was so lonely for my family and I was such a little girl. I thought I would die. Some people might think that you can't die from loneliness, but I am sure, today, that is just what that little girl was doing…she was dying." Annie watched, as she saw the old woman looking at the young girl she had been through the glass of her memory.

The woman with the gray hair pulled back around her earth-brown, rounded face continued. "She didn't laugh anymore, the little girl in boarding school. She didn't look at anyone. Colors started to disappear, and all she could see was brown floor and brown dirt outside. It was in the fall, so even the sky looked like it was dying with the little girl. It was hard for her to dress, or walk; she would just slide her feet to get to the class. I think she was almost dead."

"Then, one day she shuffled back to the coat closet to get her coat. When she picked up the coat, it felt heavier than when she had hung it up. She thought maybe it was because she was weaker, still, than when she had first come in but, as she lifted the heavy coat to put it on, she put her hand in her pockets. She felt something very big."

"The little girl pulled the huge smooth thing from her pocket and woke up when she saw bright red. She looked around, surprised; wondering how did the apple get in her pocket? No one else was pulling an apple out of their pocket. Someone had put the apple in just hers. As she looked around, she saw a beautiful, brown, young woman, neat as a pin in an ironed white blouse, standing soft and straight, smiling at her. The little girl's whole face smiled back, as she took the loudest, sweetest, juiciest bite she had ever experienced."

"So", the old Miwok woman said, "You see me here, alive, because that was your Auntie who put the apple in my pocket. She was there all the way from Nevada and she saved my life; that was just the first time she brought me an apple. For many months, every time the little girl thought she would die from loneliness, her spirit found an apple in her pocket. Your Auntie was so beautiful, and she had such a strong smile. And, because of her, I am alive to tell you this story today. There were other people who saved my life in later years, but your beautiful Auntie was the one who saved the little girl."

"As a young girl that's what I thought. I thought she was *so* beautiful. And, here today, as an old woman, I can tell you that was true."

16

NEW PLACE

The man who raised Michael had found a small town where they could all grow surrounded by mountains that made Annie feel warm. They had been in the town for several months when Annie walked with her son in the market.

Michael had decided to give himself a dramatic Mohawk haircut. He had walked out of the bathroom one day with hair standing up in the middle of his head and both sides of the stand flanked with smooth skin. Annie and the man who raised Michael looked at each other and the man told him, "Nice job." Annie could not help but smile to herself because she remembered when he was still small, and just learning his numbers, he called the hairdo he now sported "the number one." When asked why he called it that, the answer was obvious, "Well, just look; it's a number one standing on someone's head." As they walked through the market, his hair was unshaken by his solid adolescent gait.

As they began to round the corner to grab some pickles, an old man was shuffling behind his cart. He looked up and saw Michael. "Hey, Mike, I like your haircut."

"Thanks, Bob." Michael responded.

As they moved on, Annie asked Michael how he knew the elderly gentleman. "Oh, he's just someone I met."

As the weeks went on, both Annie and the man who raised Michael became puzzled by the number of centenarians that Michael was on a first-name basis with. Michael and the man who raised him were at the hardware store, and the gas station, when two different shriveled old men stopped for conversation with him. Annie had the same experience, and when they compared notes, they were baffled because in each exchange Michael and the old men had known each other by name.

They both agreed that it was time to see what was going on. That evening when the three of them sat down to dinner (Cajun chicken, Basmati rice, and cold sliced bell pepper and cucumber) they decided to casually approach the subject.

The man who raised him addressed Michael, "Hey, Bud, we noticed that you seem to have your finger on the pulse of the Senior Citizen population in town. How did you meet all these people?"

Michael looked up from his chicken with no hesitation. "Well, we're new. I don't know a lot of people and a lot of old people are lonely. I noticed that here most of these old guys have their names tooled on the back of their leather belts. So, all I do is read the belt and say, "Hi, Bob."

"They're so glad to have someone talk to them. They usually say, 'I'm sorry, I can't quite pull your name out.' Then I tell them, 'My name's Michael' and they say 'Oh, yeah, Michael. How you doin', Mike?' For some reason most of them want to call me "Mike." They have cool stories and sometimes we just sit and talk for a long time. I like to listen and they like to talk."

So it was that it became routine for Michael to know most of the senior men in the town by name. Since he knew them by name, many assumed that they also knew him, and had just forgotten. When they talked, they remembered that they knew him, usually as one of their friends when they had been young, when they laughed easily and knew the world was simple.

It seemed as though Annie's son had just arrived in her life when he died. He lived only twenty-one years and her peace came in knowing that his living had been a treasure for her.

17

WAILING SONG

When Michael died, Annie remembered that a woman always knows what to do for the family.

She stood alone in front of the creek and, without her knowing she had asked for it to happen, she found two women standing with her.

One of the women who stood with her at the creek was a woman that she had heard about. She had lived at a time when there were Indian hunters, men looking for Indians to hunt. This woman was with a family group by the creek, hiding in the willows. The woman was breast-feeding her new baby and her baby began to cry. The young mother was frantic. The hunters were coming closer by the minute. Her other children, her Mother, her Grandmother, her nieces and nephews were all around her, crouching, every pore consumed with fear, and her new baby could not be calmed.

Annie remembered being at a Pow Wow where that woman and that baby were honored. The young mother had suffocated her baby. She held her baby's face against her breast, with tears rolling silently down her cheek until the child died, so that all of the family could live. The mother knew what she had to do.

As Annie stood by the creek, preparing to bury her son, she stood with the woman she had seen honored at another Pow Wow. She and all of her people were trying to evade the soldiers. The woman was on horseback with her baby. The river was ice cold and her horse was exhausted. Half way across the river, this horsewoman, this mother, knew that her horse could not carry her weight. She tied her baby to the horse and she allowed herself to be swept away by the icy river. Annie remembered being at the Pow Wow where all the descendents of the baby, the descendents of that woman, danced in her honor. The family had survived. They filled the gymnasium with power as the drum beat. They came onto the floor to honor the love of that mother. They were many.

Annie stood by the creek and these two women stood beside her. They told her that they had each known loss. Each woman stands where she must. Others may watch her but only her Mother and her Grandmother, and the women who have also had their children leave this world, could stand with her. These women could stand with her. They told her that she would know what to do.

They told her that as Mothers, they would be with her. The three of them stood at the creek until Annie got cold, and then numb, and then, finally, strong. Annie remembered that the whole of the family was why she was a woman. Her calling was not related only to her one precious child. The soul of the family was what she had to nurture. The soul of the family was why she was there.

Annie stood at the creek. She breathed the soft, cool drops of water that the air carried up to her from the creek. The mist, and Annie's tears, washed her face as the wind wiped her hair from her cheeks and brushed it gently from her neck. She stood on the smooth river rocks. She stood with the two beautiful spirit women beside her. Feeling someone watching her, she looked at the bank across the river. Standing tall, she looked at the cedars across the water, she looked up to the ridge of the mountain, and, at the top of the ridge, she saw Coyote. He looked down at her; she looked at him. All of her questions were answered in his look.

He knew this was not the time to joke, not the time to deceive her. He looked at her and reminded her that he was the Father of the Shoshone. He and the Creator had talked and laughed, and now they both stood with her.

Annie stood on the bank and looked into the eyes of Coyote. She could see his eyes and the soft gray hair on his cheeks. She saw his sharp ears and his solid jaw. She closed her eyes and took a deep breath. She felt the mist of the creek on her eyelids and when she exhaled she opened her eyes, and Coyote was gone. In her heart she felt his look and his knowing that she would be able to walk, in a good way, with her loss.

Her son and all of the elders and children who had come together with her, they were all the children of the Coyote.

When Michael died, Annie knew that no one should wear black. As the telephone calls went to all the Aunts, Uncles, cousins, siblings, her one request was, "I want no black." Of course, the extended family including the variety of ages and the large numbers that it did, it was easy to explain how one person somehow got the message that she wanted "no blacks." This miscommunication was especially confusing because Annie's life, and her son's, had been shared with people from every color and creed that offered to be a part of her bouquet.

One sister said that she could not help but be a little excited because her daughter had, in fact, worn nothing but black for the past several years, and she knew that out of respect for Michael and his mother, her daughter would be embraced by color for the first time in ages.

Annie's brother and brother-in-law went to get Michael in the pick-up. He had died in the city. Both of the men were from the mountains, very big and very brown, and they went, without questions, to bring Michael home.

While the guys went to get Michael, the cooking started. The smells of the cooking foods met the smells of the food brought in by family and friends. One woman brought venison roast, another had cooked a turkey. In came ham, chili, stew, cakes, pies, breads, green salads, macaroni salads, cookies, fruit, sodas, juices, and milk. The refrigerator, kitchen table and counter began to disappear under the food.

Tents went up in the back yard by the creek. To the right of the back door, a large white tent was erected. The big tent was where Michael would stay. The Uncles and cousins began to string a cord and rigged a shop light so that anyone who wanted to visit with Michael in the night would be able to see him.

Annie looked out the back door. The big white tent was on the right, framed in new spring grass. The creek ran just below it and, in the center out in the yard, the boys were beginning to stack logs and brush for tonight's bonfire. Over on the left of the bonfire was a row of smaller tents, where the cousins and Uncles would sleep, outside, with Michael. Chairs were being set up beside the bonfire. When the sun set, there would be drumming. The guys would keep the fire burning. Michael would be there with them and they would all be together till the bonfire swallowed the night and even until the day hid the power of the fire.

Michael's Uncles took him to the local mortician. Annie had asked his Uncle to bring his favorite shirt; she did not want him to be buried in something that he would have considered a fashion mistake while he was living.

The mortician asked Annie and the man who had raised Michael what they wanted in the obituary. Annie knew that all of Michael's cousins had to be named. He was leaving them and they had loved him. They had danced at Pow Wows together, ridden horses, fished, eaten, slept, laughed and listened to their family stories together. The cousins had to be named in the obituary. The mortician was a gentle man. He tried to explain that he had buried many Native Americans and he knew how important cousins were. Unfortunately, the newspaper only thought brothers and sisters were important and there wasn't really anything that he could do about it.

Annie asked him to let her think for a minute. The mortician and the man who raised Michael left her alone at the long wooden table in the room full of soft burgundy carpet. Annie remembered her Uncle taking her with him on the Reservation round-ups. She remembered Uncle stopping at the top of a huge mesa. They had both looked over the desert valley from atop their horses as they chewed on warm carrots that she had carried in the pocket of her Levi's. She remembered Uncle Ellis telling her, as they looked over the land where her family had been created, that for the Shoshone, "Your cousins are your brothers and sisters."

Annie remembered laughing with her cousins, and she remembered that the only reason she ever had a big brother, was because she had older boy cousins. In her heart she could feel the bond that Michael and his cousins had when they danced together, bustles, bells, beads, bear claws, eagle talons, ribbon, buckskin, and the power of all of their shared ancestors blessing their dance.

Annie knew what she had to do.

Annie invited both of the men back in and she asked for a paper so that she could write the names of all of her nieces and nephews. She put their own last names to honor their parents but she listed them all as Michael's brothers and sisters, so that she could honor Michael, and his cousins, and her Uncle, and her Grandparents, and all of their ancestors.

When the newspaper came out, it listed all of Michael's cousins as his brothers and sisters. There were some seventeen last names and only when it was seen in print did everyone laugh. They knew that Michael would laugh to see that to honor his family it looked, at face value, as if his mother had had children by seventeen men. Everyone chuckled but they also knew that Annie had chosen what was important.

Michael's Uncles began to build his casket. All of Michael's male cousins worked with their fathers and Uncles to make the box where Michael would lie as he waited in the tent for each of them to wish him good travel. The young men used the Skilsaw to cut the boards, the teenagers used the power screwdriver to hold the boards in place and the little men sanded the wood and brought the screws. Annie came to the porch to watch her brothers and nephews as they made this gift for her son, for her, for themselves, and she felt that something was very wrong, but at the same time, she knew that something was very right.

They felt her standing on the porch, and they sanded harder, spoke more softly, and held each piece of pine as though it were their child. She watched as something very sad and beautiful was made.

18

MONA

Annie's mother, Mona, had been trained as a nurse and she was adept at organizing. She was a beautiful, brown, eclectic woman. When Annie was young, Mona had painted a mural with oils on their living room wall. Mona carved wooden guns for her infant sons and sewed satin dresses for her daughters. She knew how to hold a sage hen by the neck and spin the body quickly until the head and body separated. In fact, Mona had been the official sage hen spinner as a young girl when she followed her brothers hunting. They would shoot the birds, she would spin them and track down the sage hen bodies that had flown into the sagebrush to put in a bag that she carried. Mona knew how to bake a soufflé, how to stitch a wound, and how to pick up a marble with her toes. She had shared a special bond with Michael.

The beauty of her relationship with this grandchild was that he completely "got her." He once bought her a small rubber chicken key chain. That key chain said, "I love your humor and your independence. I love who you really are; I love that you are my Grandmother, and I am your grandson."

One of Mona's adventures had been to take an upholstery course. She had, of course, also taken Gourmet Cooking and Finish Carpentry 101. Mona decided that she would upholster Michael's casket. Mona proposed the upholstery project to Annie.

Annie looked at her mother. This was one of those activities that would give her mother peace. Annie told her, "Michael needs to be here in two hours. We need to be sure that everyone has time with him tonight and he needs to be with all of his family, so if you are able to do this within the next two or three hours, I think it would be wonderful."

Mona went into action. She immediately telephoned a resident in the next town who had gone to Bureau of Indian Affairs (BIA) School with one of her sisters. She explained the task and gave a comprehensive list of fabrics, staple guns, glue, staples, foam, and a variety of hammers and tapes, and a tape measure.

The Indian woman in the next town would purchase all the required items and Mona sent one of her sons-in-law to pick up the materials. She stressed that time was of the essence and she intentionally selected the son-in-law who had a taste for fast driving. Mona dispatched Lead Foot, and in short order, the son-in-law's pickup had made it to town and was pulling back into the driveway. Mona ran out, accompanied by the team she had designated to help her carry everything into the back yard, to finish the casket. The team rushed to the pickup (having been told there was not a moment to waste).

Mona asked, "Where is the stuff?"

Her son-in-law looked confused. "It's all there in the back." He walked to the back of the pickup. He looked surprised. "It was all there. I just got it." The pickup bed was embarrassingly empty. There was nothing in it.

"Oh, my gosh!" Mona was on a mission and the goods were not there. "Hurry! Get someone else, you guys go look for the stuff, it must have blown out."

For the next hour, several rigs, manned by several sons-in-laws, drove up and down the highway, searching for the upholstery kit. Nothing was found. Just as Mona was about to become frantic, one of her sons came up to her and firmly tucked her under his arm, "You know, Mom, I think Michael just wants to keep it simple. We just need to let him have it his way,"

Mona heard her son and she called off the search and rescue team.

19

WHEN I GO DANCING

When Michael came home he was in the warm golden box that his "brothers" had made. He was wrapped in a Pendleton blanket; it draped over his shoulders looking like the blankets that had been worn by Indians a hundred years ago. He wore brand new blue beaded moccasins that Mona had brought for him. He had on a black and white woven linen shirt. His skin was clear and golden brown, his hair was raven-wing black, and he lay with gifts that had been given to him by different people in his circle. Michael's hands held one powerful eagle feather. He was fortunate that his family knew to take the feather out of the casket before he was buried. That ensured that Michael's spirit would not be trapped in the box.

At his feet lay the last quilt that Annie had made for him, folded and neat, the last of many his Mother had made for him. He had never slept with a store-bought blanket; his life had been warmed by a series of handmade quilts.

Two elders brought Michael tobacco to trade on his way. He had a beautifully beaded bottle filled with water beside him in case he became thirsty. Some gifts were for Michael to use, some were to say "thank you" and some were to say, "Remember me." No one person would ever know all of the items that were in the wooden box with him but Annie remembered seeing, among the gifts tucked beside her son, one rubber chicken key chain.

All night, Michael's cousins and Aunts went into the tent. Sometimes one by one, sometimes together, they went into Michael's tent. There were chairs for the older ones. Everyone belonged. Noni's little one said he wanted to go in and say goodbye to Michael. He was only three and he could not get up high enough to see him. His Grandma picked him up and took him into the tent. His little brown eyes looked down at Michael.

Noni's little one had always looked with his whole body. His mouth would open, as though he were just about to say "Ooohhhhhh" and his eyes looked like black walnuts, still in their black husks, round and shinning in a bed of brown leaves after the rain. His little neck, usually hidden by baby fat, somehow stretched and began to look like a neck.

He took everything in as he looked down at Michael. His little eyes were quiet, looking like the first time he saw a fish swimming near the bank; the little one looked and looked until, at last, he could feel the cold water coming through the fish's gills. He looked until his little lips had merged with shiny fish's mouth as it casually nipped at some morsel attached to the algae floating from the branch that hung from the bank and floated in the water. The little one's mouth nipped in unison with the fish as he looked.

As he was held up to see his cousin, he looked as he had looked the first time he really watched Porcupine walk, with the long needles and hair rocking back and forth with every step the short-legged porcupine took. He noticed the hairs rocking and looking as if they would flip the round animal over. This little one had always really looked at things.

When he was through looking, he waved his little brown hand and said, "Bye, Michael!" Then he looked eye to eye with his Grandma, and he said, "I'm done." She took him out of the tent and put him down and he ran off to face the other important things in his life.

At the time of night when just the tip of her nose would be cold, Annie finally walked with Michael's cousin, into the tent. Michael's cousin had been as his sister and had come into the world only one month before him. Now, she stood with her Aunt. The two, his cousin and his mother, were the last to be able to face this last place Michael's body had taken him. They walked into the sweet night grass and the smell of canvas. They stood together. They both looked at Michael, and they loved him, and each other, and all those around them outside the tent in the night. And the cool hand of the wind, and his cousin, the breeze, blew into the tent and stroked their cheeks. The Auntie told her niece that sometimes when temperatures drop, things can shift in a body, and there might be some movement. The niece, who hurt to her bones, was glad to hear herself giggle, there in the tent with the breeze and Michael and her Auntie Annie. They both knew that Michael had always protected them, and he would be sure that his body did not move in the night air.

Michael lay, wrapped in a new Pendleton blanket, his perfect slim fingers holding the eagle feather. And, before the two women who loved him left the tent. In the cool of the night, his mother, Annie, covered his hands with the soft woolen blanket before they left.

All night, Michael's Great Uncle told stories. He told stories that belonged to all of the people in the room, stories that made them laugh, stories that were outrageous, stories that had taken thousands of their own to the other side, stories that tied everyone and everything together perfectly, living and dead, animal and human, young and old.

Great Uncle told the stories in the old way. When he talked, all the Mountain Shoshone and the Fish Eaters, and the Pine Nut Eaters, spoke and sang through him. He would say, "This is a story told by an old woman from Ruby Valley." The story would begin "This was one of the stories told by your Grandma...This story is from an old woman from the Jarbridge Mountains."

Michael's Great Uncle had a hand drum and stick beside him. Occasionally a story's character needed to sing a song and Great Uncle would make the drum appear in his hand and beat and sing. The dozens of people who belonged to the song sat around him and felt the drum; they felt his singing reach the walls of the house and flow right through the stucco and wood, into the night, and out to Michael so that he, too, could hear the songs. As he told the stories through the night, the house filled with more and more old people, long since dead, who came to listen as their stories were passed on.

Great-nieces saw to it that Great Uncle was never without food or drink. He needed to have energy to tell the stories. Their Aunts would prod them if necessary but by midnight the young women understood the importance of their watering this great tree. They took pride in filling his water glass before it was empty. They became more beautiful as they discovered the importance of their serving him meat so that he would have the energy to share with everyone what he had brought for them. The young women began to understand that they were feeding their stories, the stories of their Grandparents, and the stories of the children they would one day have.

They all went with Michael to his funeral. The Uncles placed the lid on the smooth, wooden casket, and loaded him into the back of the pick-up. Everyone had gotten the word. Michael's mother wanted no black to be worn at the funeral and she encouraged people to wear whatever clothing Michael had most often seen them wear.

One wonderful man came in his bathrobe. Her best friend wore hot pink. In general, with the olive skins and bright colors, one would have thought that they had somehow stepped into a Polynesian wedding party. Michael's Grandpa played music of celebration on the piano, and his Uncles sang a Shoshone song. Michael's Great Uncle and Aunt sang a Shoshone warrior song.

After many people talked about Michael, and the funeral was over, they all went to the house to help Michael leave. As people ate, the discussion began. Great Uncle would lead the Ceremony. Great Uncle knew that a Spirit could leave most easily through an east door. The thing was, no door in Michael's Auntie's house faced east.

One of Michael's Uncles was delighted. He had spent most of his nearly forty years teasing his younger sister in a good-natured way. He went to his sister. "Sis," he said, bending over to whisper in confidence, "Michael has to leave the house from the east, but you don't have an east door, so we're going to have to knock a hole in the wall." Michael's Aunt looked at her brother with shock. At first she thought he was joking, but he looked entirely serious. She thought for only a moment. She knew Michael would need help to leave. Her brothers and nephews were all here, and if they knocked a hole in the wall, they could certainly build a new wall quickly. The weather was good. She looked at her brother and said, "Okay, you guys knock the wall out but just promise me you'll stay long enough to put up a new wall."

"Ha!" her brother laughed, delighted that he had tricked her once again. 'Promise me you'll put up a new wall'! "Hey Sis," he laughed, "We don't have to knock the wall out; you have an east window upstairs so we just have to all jump out!"

Her brother walked off laughing. Michael's Aunt watched her brother chuckle all the way outdoors where he met her other brothers, and she could see them laughing, too. She couldn't help but smile. She was relieved not to have the chaos of a construction project in the middle of Michael's time but she did see that she needed to speak with her Uncle to see what was needed.

Michael's Great Uncle had surveyed the situation. Everyone ate while he decided what he needed to do. Without anyone giving instruction, when the meal was done, everyone went upstairs to the bedroom with the window that faced the east. The Elder Aunties were helped by their grandnieces and nephews to climb the stairs. All of Michael's family, and some of their very close friends, came into the room as Great Uncle stood by the window that faced the east. Softly, in Shoshone, Great Uncle began to talk to Michael. He would talk in Shoshone because Michael was Shoshone, so his spirit knew the language well. Great Uncle also spoke gently in English. His voice was firm, but kind. Great Uncle told Michael that he was dead. He told him that all the people in this room were his relatives. They had all loved each other in this life. They would not forget that he was a part of the family but he needed to know that they were all here to tell him goodbye because his spirit needed to go. Great Uncle told Michael that he needed to go to dance with the stars and he told him about all the beautiful girls who were waiting for him among the stars.

Great Uncle burned Sweet Cedar and, as he burned the Cedar, he pointed to the people in the room. He pointed them out to Michael's spirit, and he identified them as people who loved him and who would now walk him out of the house and send him off.

Annie looked up and she saw her Uncle burning the Cedar. To his left, she saw her son. She looked at him and she could feel his expectation. Should he go? Did she need him to stay? She looked at him and she held back her tears because she, somehow, knew that this moment was crucial.

Michael had a basket in his hand and he looked at her. Annie pulled into her heart the strength that came from all of her relatives in the room and she looked at her son. In her heart, she told her son's soul "It is time for you to go." She held her gaze and her resolution. Then she turned as her Uncle led, with the burning Cedar, and all of Michael's relatives walked him down the stairs and out the front door.

Michael's Great Uncle waved the Cedar smoke with the eagle feather to send Michael on his way. Then he blessed all of his relations with the smoke.

And Michael was gone.

20

POW WOW

Annie's family knew how to move gracefully in grief, in part, because they had known how to move together already. They knew how to dance together.

One wonderful summer, Annie and a number of family members were attending a Pow Wow. As usual, as at many Native American gatherings, people introduced themselves in relation to their ancestors and indigenous territory. As one Aunt explained, "Who I am can only be understood in terms of who and where I come from, both for myself, and for those who meet me. It will be the same with you and your children."

At the Pow Wows the children, "the cousins," all danced in Native American tradition. The smiles and laughing and feathers and fringe and luggage were constant companions when they would get together for these occasions.

It was not unusual for one or more to have come several hundred miles, at fair expense, to encourage the children to spend time together with their elders and to dance.

As Annie rode in the van with the women in her family, she let various memories of previous Pow Wows pass through her mind like the scenery on the side of the highway. They had all gone to Pow Wows together since the children were very small.

They would come from their jobs, different locations, different life situations, and they would descend upon the Pow Wow campground, or a hotel, where they had already made reservations. They would jump out of their vehicles wearing sunglasses, t-shirts, shorts or jeans (whatever the weather allowed). Suitcases, boxes, and brown children would pour into an area to dress for the Grand Entry.

The last Pow Wow they'd gone to, they had two sets of adjoining rooms and all the dancers dressed in one of the sets of rooms. The weather was nice, so the doors were open. The adjoining door was open and all the cousins went in and out, and back and forth, in various stages of dress and undress.

One young nephew appeared to be upset because the Eagle beak and talon on his dance staff was loose. He looked at Annie and said, "Auntie, would you fix my staff?"

Annie grabbed the staff and began to look at the construction so she would be able to best determine how to rewrap the Eagle head with leather so that it would stay. She looked closer when she thought she saw something light move in the beak. Maybe there was leather in there, too. Annie dropped the staff when she identified the movement as a maggot. "Oh my God! This thing has maggots in it!" Her nephew laughed and his little, beaming face told her that he had known full well that the Eagle had company.

"Get your Uncle to fix it!" She playfully grabbed her nephew by the neck.

One of the little jokester's Uncles grabbed the staff, chuckling, and took it outside as his nephew followed him.

Hair was being braided everywhere. Older ones braided their own hair; little ones were having their hair braided so tightly there was more than one protest that they were going to look Chinese with their eyes pulled back so tightly. Hair ties were being wrapped around the braids. Most of the hair ties were made of beadwork but some had shells, tin jingles, and they all had graceful leather ties. Strands of bells were being tied to ankles, and the room began to sing with the tin cones that were sewn on jingle dresses, which two of the cousins wore.

One of the nephews was hollering for his roach (the head-dress made of porcupine hair that stood straight up in the center of the headdress and had wonderful turkey feathers that encircled the porcupine pelt.). "Where's my road kill?" That was what he enjoyed calling his dance roach.

"Here it is." One of his little cousins waddled over with the smooth silver/black porcupine headdress and handed it to his much taller cousin.

Some of the older boys, and the young men, began to grow more serious. Annie could feel them praying. They were praying that they would dance in a good way, praying that their life would be as committed as their dance, praying that all of their relations would be proud of them. Annie could hear one praying that if they won one of the big cash prizes they would be able to help someone in their family and, maybe, have enough left over for a new pickup battery.

The feathers and dancers and bells and jingles began to load into the vehicles to head to the Pow Wow grounds in time for the Grand Entry.

As they pulled into the parking lot, they passed licenses from Washington, Utah, Montana, Wyoming, Oregon, California, and Arizona. Shiny new vans and rusted station wagons were releasing dancers, some with dramatic yellow and black paint on their faces. One woman's face was painted with a teardrop on the outside of each eyelid. One barrel-chested man got out of a Honda and placed a tremendous bear head atop his own, the rest of the bear-skin draping over his immense back. His chest was covered with a bone vest. Annie could read the tattoo on his massive arm as they drove by: "Yollonda." Dance shawls and colors that could make an Arizona sunrise jealous were streaming into the arena. Dancers were gathering for the opening Ceremony for their several days of dance competition.

The jingle of the bells owned the arena as everyone jostled for their place. Then, the drums started, and there was a moment of stillness. The procession began.

The number of drums present could often predict the size, participation, and power of the Pow Wow. Each of the large, skin drums was surrounded by a group of singers who accompanied it. Some of the drum groups had Indian names; some had English names. The announcer firmly called out the names of the drum groups as they drummed in unison. Six drums from various areas had come together for this Pow Wow. It would be a good night.

Everyone at the Pow Wow stood as the flag bearers came into the arena. One Native American man, wearing Levi's and a ribbon shirt, carried the U.S. flag. His ribbon shirt was a popular style which was modeled after the tear shirts that the Oklahoma Indians had made when they walked, and died on the Trail of Tears. Bolts of cloth had been given to the Cherokee, but no scissors. The soldiers had feared revolt and did not want to provide the exhausted Indians with anything that could be used as a weapon. So, the fabric was folded in half, and the sleeves were torn out of cloth. Tearing the fabric, created the straight lines of the shirt. The style was sometimes called a "tear shirt," in part, because of the way they were torn, and in part because of the tears that flowed at the times the shirts were originally being torn.

A tall, Indian male, Traditional Dancer, fully dressed in buckskin and wearing an impressive Eagle-feather headdress, danced into the circle beside the man carrying the American Flag. He carried an Eagle staff representing the Native American Nations. Because there were many Canadian brothers dancing, there was a Canadian Native who came in with the flag bearers carrying the Canadian Flag. The flag bearers danced in, to the beat of the drum, and stood before the judges and elders who were all seated in a row at the foldout cafeteria table.

Behind the flag bearers came the "Royalty." All those who were present in this bunch had won Native competitions, Miss Indian USA, or Tribal princesses. Any "Royalty" who had identified themselves to the registrars came in behind the flag bearers. Beaded crowns upon their heads, silken, or beaded banners across their chests, they came in with their dance shawl fringe hanging straight and formal.

The men began to come into the ring: Traditional Dancers, male Grass Dancers, Fancy Dancers. All the men danced into the ring. First came the "Golden Age" Dancers (50 and older). Then came the younger men, excited about being able to use all of the muscles they had been working on for months. After the men, in came all the teenage boys, so many fancy dancers, bells, health, and energy. Following the teens, the younger boys danced in, some as sure as the Elders, because they had been dancing to the Pow Wow drum since before they were born. They had swayed to the drum inside their Mother's stomachs for months before coming into the world. They had known the drum before they saw light.

After the men, all the women began to dance into the arena. First came the Elders, then the younger women, teenage girls, young girls, and then all of the Tiny Tots. The Tiny Tots, occasionally, still wore diapers and some, despite the fact that they were still learning to walk, somehow danced as though they were sent here to instruct all the others who had gathered.

All of the dancers came into the ring; they formed a circle. When everyone was in, the drums beat so loudly that even the earth was dancing and then they stopped, abruptly. Silence covered the standing arena. One very little, wrinkled Tribal Elder came up to the microphone. He prayed in his Tribal language, occasionally offering his own translations as it moved him. He prayed for the dancers; he prayed thanks that the travel had been good. He prayed thanks for the place in which the Pow Wow was being held. He prayed for the young men and the babies and the families. He prayed for those families who had recently lost loved ones, in particular those who had passed on since the last Pow Wow. He combined prayer and tribute, reminding the Creator how those who were now with Him had danced. The little, old one prayed thanks for those who had organized the Pow Wow and for those who were involved in the Tribal governments. He prayed for the leaders, the teachers, and the parents. Just as the young men were about to explode with the need to dance, he wound down by reminding the Creator of who it was that was speaking. He reminded the Creator that he had not always had the walk that would have been best but, between them, he shared his thanks that he had lived long enough to "wise up."

As he completed his prayer, the arena came alive. Those in the bleachers and those with their foldout chairs on the edge of the arena began to sit. The dancers and drummers began to join in movement, and the circle of dancers began to dance in a wonderful, colorful circle, as the emcee hollered, "Inter-Tribal!"

21

NONI

On the way to the gymnasium, one beautiful niece was determined to overwhelm all her relatives with her will. Noni announced that she would not dance. Her Mother had brought her a great distance. All her regalia: her buckskin dress, moccasins, beaded purse, hair ties, earrings, bracelets, everything she wore as she danced was the result of commitment on the part of many family members. Noni was in her early teens. She knew that she was a part of something. Just like her Mother, and her Grandmother, and even her Great Grandmother Mary, Noni was a daughter of the Coyote. Out of the blue, riding to the Pow Wow, Noni stated firmly that she would not dance.

The passengers in the van, on the way to the Pow Wow, included Annie, her two sisters, the niece, Annie's Mother, and an Elder Aunt.

Upon hearing this niece's declaration, numerous female voices in varied pitch began to prod and insist that, after coming all this way, she had to dance. The beautiful girl was unbending.

For all the travelers, at various points, they somehow thought the winning argument would be pointing out to the niece that she was just being stubborn. As they persisted in trying to coax or coerce, the Elder Aunt spoke with an authority that quieted the banter.

"Leave her alone, she can't help it, she comes from 'that girl'…we all come from *that* girl."

Everyone exchanged knowing glances and stopped chirping. There is a certain authority in a voice that tells you that a story is coming.

They had all heard it before and they now heard it from the eldest child of ten…the one who had the most stories.

Even the stubborn girl in the van relaxed her stance to be attentive. She was obviously feeling victorious in having justified the telling of a story.

"This girl can't help that she's stubborn. A long, long time ago there was a young woman who was very beautiful. A long time ago people would have to travel a long way to get together and meet people, just like now. We traveled and lived in bands of mostly family members so, to marry and meet potential suitors, families had to get together and have *big times.* Sometimes they traveled for days."

"It was also a custom that a young man would see someone he liked for a wife and, later, he would come back and steal her. It was not like kidnapping would be now; it was a custom, and very exciting."

"Well, the girl, from whom we all come, was spotted at one of those get-togethers, and a young man came to steal her. He threw her on his horse and rode away from her family's camp."

"They rode for several days and, as the time passed, this girl became no fonder of the man and his horse. As they rode, this girl determined that this person (his tribe was named with contempt) would not be her husband."

"Late in the night, after several days' ride, that girl snuck away and began to walk home. She walked by herself."

"There were bears and cougars and spirits in the mountains and in the desert, but she walked and slept, and walked and slept, determined that she would choose her own way. She would not stop because she knew for herself, and for all generations, she needed to do this."

"We know that she made it. We know that she eventually agreed to marry a good man, because here we all are. And we are all that way, and we all come from that girl."

It was evident that Annie's niece, Noni, apparently inherited whatever it was that came from "that girl." Her eyes were always filled with a combination of fire and smoke. She was bound for adventure but she knew to watch and see how she might throw someone off her trail.

In her adolescence, Noni began to frighten everyone in the family with her stubbornness. She went to the fairgrounds when it was used as a barracks for all the firefighting teams who had come to put out fires that were plaguing the surrounding mountains. She had been told not to, and she had an incredible sound of innocence when she stated that she had just gone to look for her Uncles, just in case they were among the crews.

There was the possibility of truth in Noni's story. Her Uncles did fight fire. Even her Great Uncles had been firefighters. They were all smokejumpers, and the way that they understood wood and fire was renowned. Annie could remember when her own Uncles used to leave the Reservation in "The Death Trap," everyone aware that they were going to jump into fire. There was no fear about their jumping; there was no fear that they would not know what to say to the fire. But there was always a blanket of community anxiety when they took off in the dilapidated plane that took them to the far corners of the country to save the land. The Death Trap (which was what the plane was called) had a terrible habit of coughing, uncontrollably, when it was asked to take the men somewhere to fight fire. The whole of the community listened with one ear as the plane's engine would start and stop, once it had made it into the air. Sometimes there was no engine sound for what seemed an eternity and the desert air would wait for the community to breathe. Then the rusty engine sound would break the silence and people, who were pretending not to notice, took their collective breath.

Usually, only the teenage boys actually watched the plane as it occasionally took dramatic dips in elevation with each silence. If the smokejumpers had been called ahead of time, some early morning take-offs would find the boys sitting on the rails at the rodeo grounds, laughing, when the plane looked destined to nose dive, and cheering, when the engine healed. Some watched with hearts pounding hoping that, next year, they would be in the plane.

The Death Trap would circle the whole of the Reservation, sometimes four or five times, before it would stop coughing enough to take the men where they needed to go. Everyone, both on the plane and on the ground, agreed, if anything were ever to happen to the firefighters, it would not be through their firefighting. It was more likely that they would not make it *to* the fire, or would not make it home, in The Death Trap.

By unspoken agreement, The Death Trap circled the Reservation until it sounded as though it could make the flight. Without discussion, everyone knew if the plane went down, if the smokejumpers died, it would be better if it happened at home. The pot-lucks could start right away, and the souls of the Smoke jumpers and their families would have very little time apart.

The relationship between the men in Annie's family and fire even extended to those still in diapers. Annie's nephew, "Little One," was just a toddler. He was at that place where he sometimes still wore diapers because his mother needed time to say good-bye to her baby but he had conversation, and occasionally gave advice as he stood in his place between baby fat and leanness.

One day, as Annie and her sisters sat at the kitchen table talking and laughing, simultaneously they froze. Annie's sister said with fear and knowing, "I smell smoke!"

As one body, the three women, who had slept in the same womb, stood up and raced for the kitchen door.

Just outside the door stood Little One with a pile of Pecan and Oak leaves softly blazing in front of him. He stood, diapered, long legs, holding a hose and wearing a bright, red, plastic fire hat.

One sister grabbed the hose Little One had poised beside the fire. While the other sister stomped on the leaves, which were threatening to wander, his mother scolded, "Little One! What were you thinking?"

His little face held a definite frown and the look of intolerance. One could see the authority of the man who would appear in his eyes many years later. "I don't know why you're upset," he chastised his Mother and Aunties with surprising calm, "It was a controlled burn!"

Seeing Little One defend his playing with fire, Annie could not help but think of her niece, Noni. Annie was beginning to fear for Noni. She could often be found where she did not belong. A greater fear came in knowing that Noni's strength and svelte athletic body could easily invite more trouble than she had bargained for.

One evening Annie prayed for Noni. When she woke, she had a story for Noni that she knew she would have to tell her the next time they met. Noni came by that afternoon.

Annie told her that she needed to sit down because she had something for her. She made her a tuna sandwich, put it on a plate with a handful of barbeque chips, got her a soda (Noni was lactose intolerant) and, without any further exchange, Noni began to eat, looking at her Aunt expectantly.

So Annie told her the story that she had been given to tell her.

22

THE MUKUA

Once upon a time there was a beautiful girl-woman (she was at that stage of being a girl-woman, as all of us are when we are past the point of being only a girl). The girl stays inside for all of the blossoming of the female creatures, just like a diamond in a mountain.

The beautiful girl-woman had a magical power. It was called her *"Mukua"* (that's a Shoshone word for the soul… it's on the top of the head). Everyone could see it from the time she was a very little girl. She didn't see it because it shone around her head. Other people could see it because it gave her the appearance of a perfect hill with the morning sun coming up behind it. As bright as her *Mukua* was, the little girl-woman didn't know that it followed her everywhere she went. She didn't know that it made her very strong.

Of course, there were many people who admired the little girl-woman and her *Mukua*. Very often they were old people, or other people who were strong, because they knew that it was rare and beautiful for the little girl-woman and her *Mukuas* to be so connected. Like a wild sunflower in the wind, the *Mukua* shone like a dew-painted blossom, soundly attached to the stem, dancing (when the air pushed her) rather than falling over.

There were some, very often children of weaker people, who were jealous of the little girl-woman and her *Mukua*. Even though there were a few times when the little girl-woman was hurt by their envy, she still shone everywhere she walked. But she didn't yet know it.

Then, one day the little girl-woman woke up and something was different.

When the little girl-woman went to the pond to wash her face, she noticed for the first time that there was a bright glow around her head. She could not feel it on her head but it seemed to her like a bothersome spirit that she could not get away from.

As she looked in the pond, she moved her head to the left and the light stayed attached.

She reached up her left hand and felt. She could feel nothing but she could see, clearly, in her reflection that the brightness was still there. She was confused. She stood up on her feet; she could feel the gravel and smooth wet stones under her feet. She bent down and took both hands and shook and shook her hair.

Again she knelt down and looked at the reflection. The *Mukua* was still there but it had moved further to the front of her face. Now she could see it in front of her and she was angry because it felt as though it was in her way. But, in the deep part of her stomach, she felt something else. She was a little excited because, for the first time, she *knew* that she had this thing. She was excited even though she didn't know what it was.

The little girl-woman straightened her hair and decided to go and see what other people thought. She went to her parents and waited to see what they would say. Her parents had always seen her *Mukua* and had always loved her. That day, they saw that her *Mukua* was further in front. When they saw the girl-woman's eyes, they knew that for the first time she knew that she had it. Both of her parents could see that the girl-woman was testing them to try to find out what her *Mukua* could do to people.

The parents sat down and gently asked the girl-woman to sit down so they could talk to her about what had happened. They could see that she did not completely understand, and they knew that her *Mukua* was very powerful. She could see that in their eyes they had fear. What the girl-woman did not know was that their fear was for her because the most important thing for a female creature who has a strong *Mukua* is that she be humble, because it is a Gift, and not everyone has it. One cannot boast about something that one did not make and be safe.

As the girl-woman walked, there were some who did not notice. Many of them were people who were weak and they never looked long enough at anything to see when something was special or different.

The girl-woman walked all day. Some people had that look of fear but they did not talk with her about it. There was one woman the girl-woman encountered who lifted her hands when she saw the girl-woman and she pulled a globe of light from behind her own head. The woman took the light and threw it, as hard as she could, at the girl-woman. It hit her so hard that it knocked the wind out of her and pushed her to the ground. When the little girl-woman got up, she was angry. The woman was gone and so was the globe of light, but now she knew that there were other women who had them, and she was a little afraid.

The girl-woman pulled her hair. She shook her hair. She jumped up and down. Then she felt something cool and soft on the side of her face. It felt gentle, like an old woman's cool hand when a small child has a fever. The girl-woman stood very still and she lifted her left hand up to her cheek where the beautiful feeling was. She could touch it. She slowly got hold of it. She could move it. She stood as straight as a pine tree and she threw it. The *Mukua* flew through the air and tore down the trees and burned the grass that it touched. Then, so fast that it knocked her down, it flew back to her.

For several days the girl-woman walked and experimented, throwing her *Mukua* and knocking her relatives over with it. The relatives all talked with each other. They were getting bruised up but they had always known that she had it, and they always loved her. They were also afraid that she would not be able to control where she threw it. Maybe someone's house would burn down; someone might get too jealous. They feared that there could be those who would hurt the little girl-woman because they did not have a *Mukua* as powerful or bright.

There had always been strong *Mukuas* in the female creatures in her family. They all remembered how it had been for them when they had discovered theirs. All those women laughed and felt sad at the same time.

The men who had grown up with the women who had a strong *Mukua* knew enough to stay out of the way; and they knew enough to be ready to duck when they saw her getting ready to throw her *Mukua*. They did worry for her, though, because they knew that there were many male creatures who did not grow up with women who had a strong *Mukua*. They were afraid that those men would try to make her see that they were stronger and hurt the little girl-woman's feelings because they did not understand.

One day, the girl-woman woke up, and she felt very different. Her mouth was dry, all her bones ached, her neck hurt, and her face was hot. She had never felt so weak in all of her life. She could not get up. She was confused…waking and sleeping, waking and sleeping, seeing things in a cloud and unable to get up.

All her relatives were worried. They had known that a *Mukua* is not meant to be lifted and, certainly, never thrown at people; but, they knew that sometimes it would happen when a child-woman tried to discover what it could do. Some of the women in the family cried and remembered one girl-woman who had blown herself up when she threw her *Mukua;* it ricocheted off of a mountain and came back to her with such force that she turned into nothing but little pieces of light.

The women took her into a tent and lay her on a rabbit-skin blanket. They smoothed her hair and washed her face.

One by one the women in the family with the strong *Mukuas* went in to talk to the very sick girl-woman. In between sleeping and waking and being weaker than she had ever been, the girl-woman listened to their songs that told about things that their *Mukua* had done.

One woman sang a song about a time that she had been walking alone with her baby girl-child and a bear had come onto the road. The mother was afraid. The bear stood up in front of them, facing them and growling with a low, hungry sound. The woman told how she felt a gentle touch all around her and then she realized her *Mukua* had covered her and made her and her beautiful child invisible to the bear. The bear, confused because he could no longer see them, went on down the mountain and the two female creatures could continue safely.

Another woman sang a song about how her *Mukua* taught her to heal, how the lessons were very hard but her *Mukua* helped her to learn and then put magic in her hands that made people well when they were sick.

Another woman relative came in and sang a song about how her *Mukua* made men strong. She told how, when she had been a child-woman trying to learn how to use it, she would confuse male creatures, make them cry or make them angry, make them blind so they did not know where they were going. Then, when she learned how to use it, men she touched became builders and hunters and healers.

One Great Aunt came in and sang a song about her child who had died; she sang about how the pain of that loss had crippled her, and made her unable to walk. She softly sang about how her *Mukua* picked her up and helped her to walk again and, then, taught her to run like a healing wind.

One by one, the women came in. One by one, they sang about how their *Mukua* had taught them to paint, or tell stories, or make foods that strengthened travelers, and helped those who ate it to become better teachers, better students.

With each story the women sang, the girl-woman got stronger. As she could see more clearly, with each story, the lights encircling the women's heads became brighter.

The girl-woman felt stronger with every verse. The song was as clear as the first bullfrog on a quiet summer night. The girl-woman filled her lungs with air that felt like the air of a mountain dawn: clean and strong. She stood up and was surprised to hear that she, herself, knew the song the women were singing. She was surprised at how well she knew the sounds and the words but then she forgot her surprise and noticed how healthy she felt and how powerful and how humble to be singing this song with these women. She felt humble when she noticed that her feet did not touch the ground.

All the women came out. They were singing. The male creatures could tell that they no longer needed to duck. Some people looked jealous but none of the women with the strong *Mukua* were bothered by it; they were healing each other and the air with their song.

The girl-woman swayed and sang. She didn't even give a thought to the bright light all around her head because of all the brightness that radiated, all around her, from all the women with the bright lights from the strong *Mukuas*. She did not try to remove it or throw it at anyone because she knew that it was her teacher and would make her strong. It was a gift.

As the women with the strong *Mukuas* sang together, they felt very powerful, and humble, and healed.

Noni had only eaten half of her sandwich, her arm stretched out on the table, her head on her arm. She quietly blinked when she looked at her Aunt. Annie smiled at her and put her hand on Noni's cheek, "Now finish your sandwich."

Noni was like Annie, and like her Great Grandma, Mary. As a young woman she began to dream. One night she dreamed a fire and children burning. She called and talked with Annie because she felt sick and confused. Annie explained that it was her job to pray; more than that she could not do. In town, Noni heard agony in the conversations when people, everywhere, were talking about a house fire that had occurred "just last night." All of the children in the poor family had died. Noni felt dizzy when she got home.

Annie called and they talked. Annie, trying to be casual, explained that as Noni got older, it would be like having more channels on a television set. Many more things, deeper things, would come to her. Annie explained to Noni that she would know many more things than she wanted. Noni, exhausted, told her Aunt, "I don't think I'm ready for cable T.V."

Annie knew where Noni was walking. Perhaps, because they were both the same, Annie was the first to hold Noni's baby. She held the little one before he was born. In a dream, Annie felt herself holding a baby in warm water. Everything in the dream was enveloped with water that was the temperature of a lullaby. She looked at the baby in her arms and she knew that it was one of their own. As she looked, for an instant in her dream, she questioned…this baby was too thin to be one of theirs. As she thought that, she smiled; she knew the baby was skinny because he had not been born yet. She rocked him as she held him surrounded by the warm water. She hummed and held him and she knew this was her niece's baby.

When Annie woke, she called Noni. She asked her, "Are you pregnant? I had a dream about a baby and I wondered if it's your baby."

Noni laughed, "Is this how my Mother is trying to find out if I'm pregnant?"

Annie assured her that this was not some covert investigation on behalf of her Mother. She told Noni about her dream and assured her that, because of the way the news of her pregnancy came, she would not say anything to anyone. Noni told her, "Yes." She was pregnant.

Eventually that baby was born. When Noni handed baby Louis to her to hold, Annie felt as if she had held him forever. When Annie held him, his little obsidian eyes looked up at her with recognition. "Remember me?" She asked him. As his tiny face looked up at her, she told him. "I'm the Great Auntie who held you before you were born."

23

GETTING UP

For months after Michael died, Annie was tired. She was tired of knowing who she would lose, who she would love, and who could not be trusted. She was tired of seeing events and truths that others didn't see, wouldn't acknowledge.

Annie spent months walking in the mountains, watching her feet trying to feel the ground. Hearing the hawk parents' cry when they taught their children to fly, Annie watched the seasons and talked with her son and her Grandmother and the man who had raised Michael.

The older nephews took turns coming to stay with her, chop wood, help with projects, look through photo albums. She knew that they also came so she could hear them call her Auntie. Annie's Aunts, who had lost sons when they were young, called her frequently. Her mother came to stay for a time. The family said, "You are Michael's Mother, you are an Aunt, you are a niece, you are a sister, you are a daughter. And you are a woman.

The day that Annie began to feel strong again, a neighbor and friend brought an ad for a position that was open in a new Alternative Health Clinic. She told her, "You have to go apply for this. It is your job."

Eight months after Michael had died, Annie interviewed for the job. It was on her birthday. She knew on the way home that something important was going to happen. She was too weak to be entirely excited, but she said, "I see you have something for me to do."

As she drove down her dirt road to the job interview, a Coyote crossed her path. She slowed down to be sure that she wouldn't run into him. She was tired and she pushed her foot, gently, on the brake, vaguely looking at the Coyote. She was driving as if in a dream until, as she stepped lightly on the brake, she saw the Coyote wink at her before he ran into the brush. When he winked, I knew it was time to get up. All of my relatives spoke with his wink.

By the time I got home, there was a message on the phone asking if I would be able to start at the Clinic the next week. I had the job.

24

WALKING IN GRANDMOTHER'S KNOWING FIELD

For months, I had been reading the work of a scientist, a biologist by the name of Rupert Sheldrake. His writing was intriguing because he talked about something he called a "morphogenetic field." Dr. Sheldrake was from London. Sheldrake was beginning to talk with another man, a psychologist, an elderly German man by the name of Bert Hellinger. Hellinger had been talking about something that he called the "knowing field." I would never have heard of Bert Hellinger but the work that he was developing invited a man by the name of Hunter Beaumont to translate Hellinger's method into English. Hunter carried the work (as it was called) into the English-speaking world, translating books, translating Hellinger's work, and bringing the work himself wherever he went. These men were all "academics," and many people in the white world found them credible.

The method Hellinger had been developing was being used to increase the flow of love in family systems. He found that if a group of people came together (even strangers) with the intention of supporting love, information would emerge that promoted healing for individuals and families. One by one, persons were invited to do their family work.

One person would describe where they had difficulty in their relationships or how tragedy had repeatedly befallen their family. The client would be directed by Hellinger to ask other participants in the room to stand as representatives for individuals in their family. I felt at home as representatives were placed to represent the living and, also at times, the dead. There was, in the work, a "knowing." The ancestors spoke and loved their descendents. Family was "related" even at the level of the soul. Hellinger called it Phenomenology. It meant that people in a family system were connected. Now that it had a name in English, it could begin to be true outside of the Indian community and might not have to be a secret.

I loved reading about Rupert Sheldrake's ideas. He encouraged people to wonder how the geese knew how to fly together; he asked, how did they all know when to turn? I couldn't help but wonder if he knew the story about the love of Goose and Abalone Woman and the reason that Goose could not stay with her all year round (a nasty break-up which resulted in Goose getting visitation rights which ensured his visits back to the coast every year.) Sheldrake talked about dogs knowing when their owners were on their way home. I read that he had even videotaped dogs and tried to trick them by having the owners leave at different times, or drive cars that sounded different, or use different methods of transportation to come home. Many of the dogs on the videotapes still prepared to greet their owners at the door the minute their master left from work.

Sheldrake even referred to indigenous people. He did not seem to think learning should just be for some people, and he reminded us that the best science would come when everyone was invited to participate. Hellinger did not speak often of Tribal people having longstanding traditions which involved the "knowing field," but he had worked with the Zulu people in Africa for many years, so I had to assume that he knew.

What both of the men talked about was a kind of connectedness of people, families, and ancestors. They talked about Grandmother, whether they knew it or not, and they had respect.

Both seemed to know about the invisible being real. It was new to hear such a thing from non-Indians, in particularly those who had anything to do with education. These men, each in their own way, talked about everyone having a right to belong. I could sense that each of these men (had they been there) might have let Grandma Mary come into the room, nearly one hundred years earlier, when she had not been allowed to come in to see the books.

Something was moving in my life. It felt as quiet as the purple net on the Alfalfa and as powerful as the pull of the Water Babies. Exploring these academic concepts, which honored the invisible, I felt like Coyote was smiling with me.

Shortly after I came to the clinic, a beautiful woman who danced when she walked came to teach this new way of healing that was coming out of Germany. She invited people to come and observe. The Clinic Director, who had eyes like magic, told me that I would be welcome to train in the method, if I was interested. The work that was being presented was that same work I had been investigating. It was the work of Bert Hellinger. The teacher knew of Rupert Sheldrake, and she also knew about the importance of the ancestors, and, she made a place in the room for the Spirit of my Grandmother, Mary.

The Doctor who had offered the training had eyes that laughed and glittered like stars. His wife's eyes danced and, when they were standing together, their eyes seemed to twinkle in unison. If they moved, if they stood in different parts of the room, their eyes seemed like stars in the constellations that my Uncle had shown me once. Sometimes they twinkled together, side by side, like the stars on the Archer's bow. Sometimes they glittered across the room like the stars in the constellations. Always they seemed to be linked in some celestial sphere.

I went to see the introduction of the work. The instructor of the training was referred to as a Facilitator. Everyone sat in a circle, some twenty people. The Facilitator talked about all the things that I had usually had to keep secret when I was not among Indian people. The fact that the living and the dead are connected with, and influenced by, each other was talked about with an openness and respect that I had never heard from a white person. That family was connected at the level of the soul was something the Shoshone had always known.

Laced within the familiar song that I already knew were the words of the instructor, "A *constellation* is the framework for the movement of the soul. The Facilitator will identify areas that have been the source of generational stress affecting the 'soul' of the family during an interview with the client. Disorder in the family system, or interruptions of the flow of love, are acknowledged. The key focus in these constellations is: Who is *missing* in the family system? Who was disowned, incarcerated, institutionalized, or died and was never again spoken of? Who needs to be *re*-membered into the family system...into the family soul?"

I was keenly aware. The rhythm of the dominant society and the indigenous rhythm were so different. The softness of the drums that were made of hollowed logs and stretched skins were so different from the glaring copper kettledrums. In this constellations work, as the instructor spoke, it was as though the kettledrums of dominant society were beginning to beat with the quiet sensuality of the skin drums, and I could almost feel the ancestors of the two camps in the room doing the Rabbit Dance.

In the Rabbit Dance, one-two, one-two, men and women laced arms and rolled their hands as they stepped together in unison in the rhythm of men and women. I could feel the ancestors, the rhythm of people, with their partners, dancing together. One-two, one-two, they stepped together to the soft, certain beat of the Pow Wow drum, and the kettledrum followed the beat.

As the Facilitator explained the specifics of the work, for the first time in my life, I heard the drum of the white world and the drum of the native world beat completely together. As I listened with my heart, I heard the beat of the big brass kettledrum get softer and softer, until one could hear that, in fact, it was learning the song of the indigenous drum.

"The constellation will include key family members whom the Facilitator had identified during the interview. Once the key persons in the family system have been identified, representatives are chosen from the group to stand for those family members. The participant places the individuals, one at a time, in relationship to each other. At that point, the individuals standing in the roles are able to provide information that is available in the "knowing field," and the healing can begin."

The teacher explained that, in this work, everyone in the room came with intention, not an intention to control outcome but rather an intention that the soul of a family would be able to speak for itself, about what was lacking and what could change.

When everyone came with the intention to be present to support the healing in a family system, a "matrix" was created, a "knowing energetic field" from which resolutions could evolve. This was different than the "family constellation" work that I had heard of in college. That was a work where individuals would set up their family system, using representatives from the group, and a therapist would make independent conclusions about what the constellation was telling them. The constellation was the therapists' toy. They would use it to tell someone what they thought their difficulty was. The old constellations usually addressed only the immediate family, or family of origin. In this work there were other inclusions...victims of the family...perpetrators, and ancestors who were currently affecting the fate of a family or individual. In this work, I could see, the Ancestors could speak for themselves. I had always known you can trust the Ancestors.

It had always been uncomfortable for me to place great value on the pursuit of what white people called "self actualization." In the quest for total autonomy, so many of the dominant culture people felt that they were strong when they stood all alone. Those things had set me and my family, and many other Indian people, apart from that aloneness that was part of the American dream. It was a model where people had their own children and did not want to share them with Grandparents. It was a way of thinking that could not fit into my family brain.

That kind of thinking did not acknowledge each person's special place in the language. In Shoshone there is a word for Grandmother (on your Father's side) and another word for Grandmother (on your Mother's side). There is a word in Shoshone that means big brother, and a different word that means little brother. You cannot just say brother and expect someone to *know* your brother's place. The community definitions were different as well; white "cousins" were so very different from your siblings. For my family, siblings and cousins were all brothers and sisters.

The teacher shared that one principle of the work was that "Everyone has a right to belong." Within a family soul, every person who is born into that family, whole or maimed, conformist or not, has the birthright of belonging. When a family excludes one part of itself, the soul of that family suffers, sometimes for generations. As I listened to the principles surrounding this Family Constellation work, I felt again the power of a Pow Wow drum, just as I had when I was just a little girl.

As I listened to the instructor speak about the power of "belonging" that this work acknowledged in family systems, I began to think about one of my first visions of "belonging."

When I had been small enough to stand beside my young Mother, and rest my arms on her lap when she was sitting, we had gone to an American Indian Center in the city. We went to a large building with fold-out chairs and some velvet covered chairs that looked like the kind in a movie theatre.

Everyone there looked like Mom. There was beautiful warmth in the room of golden and bronze people, most with black hair and white teeth. I expected to see my Grandpa, in his scratchy red-and-black-plaid coat that smelled sweet and salty, like a warm horse blanket, and was excited to think that I might be able to have a hug from my Grandpa. The room felt that familiar.

Brown people talked and laughed, and came up the wooden stairs and into the room through wooden swinging doors that looked eager to dance. The swinging doors didn't squeak like some; they were straight and wanted to open, and then quickly spring back to welcome the next person. Soon, the people were streaming in so constantly that the doors were open all the time.

Everyone was settling. Some were sitting, some were standing, and then it came. First, there was one boom. It sounded like a clap of thunder when your head is under the pillow, deep and earth shaking. The huge drum in the corner of the room had brightly feathered people standing around it. They drummed and then began to sing together. Drumming and singing filled the room with sounds so deep and so shrill that I wanted to laugh and cry at the same time. I could do neither. All I could do was be a part of what grew inside of my heart.

The feeling that grew with each beat of the drum was stronger than the way I had felt when I had climbed all the way to the top of a huge pine tree and looked down to see both of my parents completely afraid, and I was not. Then, in an instant, everyone was a part of the drumbeat. Something changed in the room. All the hearts were beating with the drum. Everyone knew the drum and the drum knew them. The people around the drum began to sing and I was at home. And when I looked up at my Mother's face, I could see that she too was at home.

A woman came and sat beside my Mother. They began to talk. First, they identified where they had come from, their land and their people. Then, they told each other their family names. Something magical happened. The language that my mother used with her babies began to flow from her lips and from the mouth of the woman beside her. They both began to speak in their own language. As they both spoke in Shoshone, they wept. They held each other's hands and they talked and laughed with tears tickling their cheeks to celebrate their meeting.

I watched, and felt the power of belonging. I also saw that it could make you cry. But something about this kind of crying was beautiful.

In this Systems Constellation Work, the lithe Facilitator spoke of my family truths with love and knowing. The teacher invited all of my relatives, and everyone's relatives living and dead, to be with us as we stood with this woman and her healing medicine.

After the beautiful teacher had spoken of the principles of the work, she quietly nodded. The room was still as her head gently bobbed while she nodded. She sat perfectly still, and then she said, as though she were whispering a prayer, "I think we start."

The teacher asked if there was someone who wanted to do a constellation; her eyes connected with a woman who was seated in the circle. The instructor nodded at her and patted the empty chair beside her. This woman was like so many Indian people and communicated with her body, and her eyes, and her heart.

After the hearts of the woman and the teacher had agreed, the tired-looking woman volunteered to come and sit beside the Facilitator. The woman talked about how she had such difficulty enjoying life. Her relationships had all failed. She had been in therapy for ten years without having any more joy than the day she had started to see a therapist. The teacher/Facilitator kindly stroked her hair and nodded.

The Facilitator asked her if anyone in her family had died or been excluded, and the woman softly shared that her father had died when she was a child. Her mother had never recovered and she had spent much of her youth alone.

The teacher asked the woman to select someone sitting in the circle to represent herself. She was told to, also, select someone to represent her mother and another person to represent her father.

Once the woman had selected people to volunteer to stand as representatives in her constellation, the Facilitator encouraged the woman to stand behind the representatives, one at a time, to quietly center herself, and listen to where each person needed to be placed within the circle. The teacher said that the person doing their constellation, and the representatives, would have a "knowing" about where they should stand.

As the fragile woman stood and placed her hands on the back and shoulders of the woman who represented her mother, she began to quietly weep. She walked the lady who represented her Mother gently to the edge of the circle, and turned her, so that she was facing the center.

She then placed the man who agreed to represent her Father. She led him into the center of the circle. After the frail woman had placed him in position, the man who represented her Father looked at the representative of her mother with longing.

Then, the little client stood behind the woman who had said she was willing to represent her. The client paused, tearfully, with her hands on the shoulders of the woman who would stand in her place, and then, with her hands on the representative's back, she began to slowly walk the woman toward the representative for her father. The woman who had been willing to stand in her place and the tired-looking little woman walked together, until the representative stood squarely in front of the representative for the father. After the woman had placed her own representative, she was kindly offered her seat and began to watch.

I felt something incredibly familiar. A "knowing field" caused the representatives of the mother and father to slowly move to face each other, yearning. Unable to cross a chasm, unable to see their daughter, the father and mother looked at each other, the living and the dead. Still bound by love, they did not notice the representative of the woman reaching for her parents with her eyes.

The Facilitator moved as I had watched so many Indian Elders move. She was dancing between this world and the next. The Facilitator gently reminded the Mother that it was time to let her husband go. The man who stood representing the Father began to be able to look at his daughter. The Father, who had died, was able to say good-bye to his wife and his child, and the room was filled with a quiet peace. When this healing dance was done, the tired woman smiled from her chair. She looked younger. She knew that her Mother and Father had shared a deep love for each other and, in the course of the constellation, she discovered that their love had extended to her, as well. Somehow, there was no more emptiness in her eyes, or her heart.

Meeting this work, I had the sense that I was remembering something that I had already known, something that had almost been forgotten. The feeling that I had, watching the Facilitator, reminded me of the Bear Dance. For many societies, the symbols of womanhood were delicate or petite. They portrayed the fragility of women, the vulnerability. For the Shoshone, the dance that celebrated the women was the Bear Dance. This powerful dance had stopped in the 1930's (when so many customs were being discontinued) when the people were too tired to dance anymore. Little by little, people began to heal. One beautiful day, in the late 1990's, the Bear Dance came back.

Only women did this Bear Dance. In couples, sisters, mothers, nieces, cousins took to the center of the floor at the Pow Wow and did a firm, beautiful, dance, each couple holding each other. At first, only the older women looked smooth and firm. They remembered the dance. Their faces were happy and sad. Many had a younger woman as a partner. With every beat of the drum they all remembered their dance: the little girls who had never had their feet feel the steps, the teenage girls who had never seen it, the Grandmothers, and Great Grandmothers; they all remembered their dance. They all remembered the mother bear, that animal woman who would protect her children, that woman who knew where to gather roots and who would teach her children to dig. That formidable woman creature who could stand her ground anywhere; *she* was the perfect symbol of womanhood. The walk of the Bear Woman, and this Bear Dance, was what tied all of these women together. As they danced, they remembered her, and they remembered their walk.

As I heard and felt the lecture about this Constellation work, my soul knew that I was remembering a Bear Dance. I knew this work and I believed Grandma Mary would know this work. As I listened, I could feel my soul and the soul of my Grandmother doing the Bear Dance, together, in the center of the circle.

The day came in the training when I was asked to facilitate. As I talked with the man who had pain that he was tired of carrying, I felt something familiar. I felt entirely awake. It was as though my entire body was made of antennae.

I remembered this feeling. It was like the times when I would run out into the field of fresh-cut Alfalfa and climb to the very top of the stacked hay bales. I would lie on the top, so high that no one could see me. I could feel the dry stems of the Alfalfa gently poke my back and arms, not quite strong enough to stab through my Levi's. I would lie with my eyes closed and could feel as though I was looking at the sun through my closed eyelids. I knew not to look directly at the sun because there was the short little blind Indian Elder who had told me that she was blind because, when she had been a young girl, she had admired the sun too much. A person could get into trouble if they admired anything too much.

When I lay on the hay bales, I could feel the land all around me. I could float above it, and I could feel all of my ancestors. I knew that I was surrounded by many people, and they were my family. Maybe some of them had been my height; maybe some of them had looked at the world with brown eyes that would have looked to me as though I was looking in a mirror. Maybe some had wide feet like mine, or strong calves too, or the same way of breathing in and smelling all the world when they were alone. My people had been there for 10,000 years, or forever. I knew that they could see me up there, on top of the hay bales, and they were glad that I was there.

When I stood as a Facilitator, I could feel the ancestors of the man who had come to have his constellation, and they were glad to see me too.

Standing in the constellation, I could feel everything.

25

LUCA

I was outside pruning walnut trees when I heard the phone ring. My nephew had been in a serious automobile accident. I had been sharing with all of my family what I was learning about the constellation work. They all knew that it was working with ancestors; the constellation work recognized that sometimes a person has a destiny, but that sometimes, things can happen because there are other forces at work. It was such a curiosity to the family that a group of non-Indians would be looking at other forces that usually went unnoticed by people who were outside of the Indian community. In fact, these outside forces, and the participation of ancestors, was something that they usually only talked about among themselves because those conversations about ancestors were among the kinds of concepts that people many native people had been beaten, and humiliated, for.

The concept of being connected to ancestors, and the dead, had been one of those areas defined as "savage." Now that a European psychotherapist was talking about it, some of the white world no longer thought it "primitive."

Everyone in my family understood the concept that there could be ceremonies which would shift the energy, and change the events in someone's life, for the better. In my heart, I thought of the work as Ceremony.

As he lay in the hospital, I asked my nephew if he wished to have a constellation done on his behalf, a constellation by proxy. My nephew, who was already aware of the work, said that he would. He said that he wanted his Uncle, the man who raised Michael, to place the representatives on his behalf.

I spoke with the Facilitator and explained the nephew's serious condition. Everyone in the family was worried for Luca because he had faced a number of other catastrophes. Luca had suffered several serious injuries and accidents. He had broken an ankle just prior to being able to attend college. It was not unusual for this hard-working young man to be sidetracked by unforeseeable misfortunes, often in the form of accidents. Preceding his inexplicable challenges, Luca had lost several close relatives, Michael, other cousins, an Uncle, all so young, had such tragic and sudden deaths.

The Facilitator listened as all in attendance "held the space." After a period of silence, the Facilitator asked that two representatives be placed. One representative would stand for Luca; the other representative would stand for Death.

The man who raised Michael carefully placed two participants from the group of people who had come together in the circle. They faced each other, standing some eight feet across from each other. One man stood as a representative for Death and the other stood as a representative for Luca.

Death looked at Luca with intensity, attempting to will his full attention. Luca, diverting his eyes, made every effort to avoid the gaze of Death. Death, being ignored, began to move slowly toward Luca.

The Facilitator explained, "In constellation work, one of the things we have learned is that a representative who stands for Death does not move. Death does not walk toward us; we move toward death. Death does not look at us because Death serves another Master." Knowing this, the Facilitator interrupted the steps of Death. The Facilitator stated, pointing at the representative for Death, "This is not Death. The "knowing field" has turned this representative into another being. This representative has become The Dead."

The Facilitator asked if Luca had experienced the loss of family; I recounted the circle of young men who had died around Luca. As many Indian people have, Luca had been quietly injured by deaths and loss since his earliest days. He also knew the losses of his parents, and their parents, and he sometimes felt the loss of the whole valley when he drove by himself on the Reservation.

The Facilitator instructed the representative for The Dead to come and to lie before Luca. The representative lay on the floor, several feet in front of Luca's representative. The intensity of the gaze did not diminish. Now, as "The Dead," the desire for Luca's focus was apparent. The representative for the Dead looked at Luca as if to pull him in with his eyes.

Luca was almost exhausted in his effort to avoid the attention of The Dead. The Facilitator stood before The Dead and instructed The Dead to state: "I now know that I am dead". After the representative for The Dead spoke those words, the representative for The Dead gave an audible sigh of relief. The tension of the gaze subsided, somewhat, but Luca was still aware of the eyes of The Dead upon him.

The Facilitator noted that The Dead was still looking at Luca. Gently turning the face of The Dead away; the words, " And I leave you now" were given for The Dead to speak. After the head of the representative for The Dead was turned away from Luca, the man who stood as the representative for Luca visibly relaxed.

In a final movement, The Dead was instructed to say, "And now I have peace." When those words were spoken, the eyes of The Dead closed. The energy in the room seemed to actually shift to a feeling of peace.

I called Luca. I told him about the constellation and he gave me permission to share it with his Mother, and his Grandmother, on the Reservation. When the constellation was shared with several of his extended family members, it was decided that it was important for Luca to have a Ceremony to confirm, for himself and The Dead, that they each had their own place. Mona made the calls and the prayers and sage and sweats affirmed that Luca's place was in the land of the living; the dead could have their peace.

The accidents stopped. Luca's lonely walk became more firm. When his body was healed, the family had a wonderful Pow Wow and give-away, to thank the Creator for helping Luca to learn to walk firmly with so many of his male cousins already walking in the other world, his heart connected to his brothers on the other side, he could feel his body, and his soul, say, "This is where the Creator wants me to be". At his Honor Pow Wow, Luca danced. He danced: Traditional, Chicken Dance, Duck and Dive, and Men's Fancy Dance, and he danced, thankfully, on the earth, while his cousins danced on the other side, beside him.

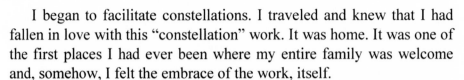

I began to facilitate constellations. I traveled and knew that I had fallen in love with this "constellation" work. It was home. It was one of the first places I had ever been where my entire family was welcome and, somehow, I felt the embrace of the work, itself.

When I facilitated constellations for Tribal people, they too felt some peace in the way the work recognized them. They often had insights into the work that clarified the discoveries of the "Creators" of this discipline. It was simple. When Native Americans, and Constellation work came together, it was simply "Ceremony".

One of the concepts in the work was the removal of a murderer from the circle of the family. At times, when some ancestor had perpetrated a heinous act, murdered or victimized many people, the representative of that individual would be placed outside of the circle. The circle of people who had come to support the constellation work represented the circle of life, the place in which people are engaged and committed to seeing what there is that Life would ask of them. Physically, it looked in the constellation as if the person was being exiled. One of the natural laws identified in the work was that "Everyone has a right to belong." There seemed to be a conflict. If there was an ancestor who had murdered, their representative was placed outside of the circle, separated from the group. The placement was described as the individual being given over to the "greater soul". At times it looked like, "You're outa here!"

One constellation in a Native American group involved such a removal. Even the remorse of the representative for the murderer did not allow the other representatives standing in the circle to feel safe. The person who represented the murderer was asked to leave the circle and face away from the family. The "murderer" was gently directed by the Facilitator to turn away from all of the representatives in the circle who were standing for the "family." He turned his back toward the "family representatives" who were still standing in the circle.

When the representative of the murderer was removed from within the circle, and turned away, everyone left standing in the constellation sensed peace and calm. When the constellation was complete and everyone sat down. There was a moment for reflection. The Facilitator explained that this dynamic did not happen often. What happened most of the time was that the living and the dead would reconcile.

For the group of Tribal people, to remove someone from the group had such historic and horrible consequences, that the discomfort in the room was thick. I could see people weighing the benefit of the murderers isolation from the group against the pain of the separation.

There was some relief in hearing that this separation did not occur often in a constellation. Everyone had heard of people who had accidentally killed someone: drunk, in an auto accident, in a jealous rage, things happen that no one could judge. Family was still family.

After some time, one beautiful young man, who had spent much of his time with elders, quietly spoke. He shared with the group an acorn story.

26

THE ACORN STORY

"**W**hen I saw that person being put outside of the circle, I thought about it and I hurt for him for a minute. Then, I thought of our acorns."

"Our people have always gathered acorns. We leach the nuts; run water through them in several ways to take the bitterness out. Different tribes leach the acorns in different ways. The Indians in Happy Camp used to gather the acorns and make boxes that they would put in the creek in the fall. All through the fall and into the winter the creek would leach the acorns. In the spring when you took the acorns out, and let them dry, they were sweet. An old man from Happy Camp told me about that. He is the same old man who also told me the story about the way he used to hunt and carry the deer home when he was just a boy."

"The old man told me that when he would hunt, and when the old ones hunted long ago, if they got a deer they would skin it out. If they were alone and had a long way to walk back home, they knew how to carry their deer. They would skin the deer and take off the neck roast, the hams, the back-strap, most of the meat of the deer and they would use the hide as a sack. They would put the meat in the middle of the hide, gather the four leg parts of the hide, and hold them. It made a good sack, they could use it to carry the deer meat home if they were alone and on foot."

"Anyway, different Tribes had different ways of getting the bitterness out of the acorns. For some of us, we would dry them, pound them into flour and they would be leached in a special basket.

Water would be poured over the acorn meal in the basket, again and again until it was sweet."

The young man had everyone in a trance as he spoke with a soothing melody in his voice, quiet, strong, and calm. He looked at the eyes of the people watching him and he decided to wake them up. He fed them something for their cognitive mind. "They say the bitterness of the acorn comes from the tannic acid. That's what we're actually leaching from the acorn."

Again he relaxed and began to sing them the rest of the story, "When we used to gather acorns, and today when we do, we often have to put them in a sack or a bag, and then we keep them while they dry. Nowadays, we put them in a paper sack; in the old days, when they had been dried a little bit, they would be put in baskets or leather bags."

"When we are through gathering the acorns, we have to look at each one to see if there are any worms that have gotten into that acorn. You look for little, tiny holes on the outside of the thin shell or sometimes there's just a big hole and you see the worm right there. If we keep the wormy acorn with the rest of the acorns, they will all go bad; they would all be at risk of being ruined. When we find such an acorn, we put it aside."

"When we are through sorting the acorns, we take the wormy ones and we pray over them. We thank the Creator for making them and we honor that the life of those acorns took a different path. We take those acorns and we give them to the earth. We don't say that they're bad, we just know that they could harm the other acorns; we give them to the earth because she is able to take care of them."

"That's what I thought of when I saw the person who represented the murderer being taken outside of the circle. The acorn is still a part of the acorn family, but it might be too dangerous to stay with the rest of the acorns. It is still a part of the acorn family, it could never be anything else."

The Indian people in the group listened and nodded. Those who had relatives who were not safe for the family remembered that they were still a part of the family. They could never be anything else.

27

HEALING TIME

There was a man who facilitated Family Constellations and I trusted him. It was certain for me that he also often "knew" things but he did not know how to be with that. He could see what was there but he was clumsy, at times, because no one had taught him what to do with his sight. He often said, loudly, that there was "no such thing as intuition" but I knew that he only said that because he was white, and afraid, and gifted with the ability to see things from this world and the next.

Once I had heard that in Europe there had been midwives who had legendary "knowing." They never missed a birth. Miles away, through rain or snow, regardless of what phase the women were in their pregnancies, these magical mid-wives "knew" the time of delivery. They would arrive at the door at the necessary moment. Unfortunately, much of those "knowings" eventually threatened their lives. Witch burnings and inquisitions led the gifted descendents of these women to hide from their own gifts. Perhaps this man was one of those descendents in hiding.

Sometimes this knowing man was like a child who wanted all the toys to be his. Not seeing his Father, or Mother, or the maker of the toys, he loudly believed he was his own owner and Creator. Then there were times that he would be like a generous child, spontaneously giving all of his toys away. Giving, and seeing the joy in people's eyes, he would be spurred on in his excitement, to give everything away and then, sadly, he would notice that he was left with nothing.

What I knew was that when he facilitated a constellation, he could stand and be fully with someone in pain. He would stand like a warm rocky mountain bluff that they could lean and rest against. Those were times when I could see that he was a man who had come from good men. I could see his feet on the ground and all of his ancestors standing behind him.

I heard that he was going to be doing a Constellation Workshop in a town nearby. When I knew I could no longer bear the weight of my pain, I asked this man, this clumsy man with the right heart, if he would facilitate my constellation. He was not afraid. In the workshop he directed me to put up those representatives who would most effectively provide answers to my questions.

He facilitated a constellation that showed the loss and the love, that I could not change. When the constellation was finished, I left the room and drove, in the dark, to the room where I would sleep.

As I slept, I heard the voices of old Indian women singing. That night, after my constellation was done, I heard the songs. Soothing, healing, pounding and prevailing, I heard old Indian women sing. These were the golden skinned women who had survived every eventuality of love, and life, and death. As I slept in my bed, warm and fully given to exhaustion, I heard them all singing.

These were the women of my family. They held me, and they sang, and they took me into the safety of the cave. Singing and holding, singing and rocking, stroking my hair, they sang to me that night. In the cool quiet of the cave they sang. As they sang, even with my eyes closed, I could feel Coyote as he lay at the door of the cave. He was watching me and all of the women who knew the song about loss.

The next morning, when I woke, I felt more solid and whole than I had in months. I drove home through miles of wheat fields. At one point in the highway I had to stop for a four-way stop sign. I looked in every direction; the coast was clear. I began to cross the road, but paused because I felt someone looking at me. I looked to the right, and there on the side of the road (where I had looked just a second before and seen nothing) stood Coyote. He and I looked at each other and then I smiled at him. Coyote nodded his head and crossed the road, headed in my direction. I put my little car in gear and crossed the road after him and waved at him as I drove by.

When I got home, I worked in the yard, took the dog for a walk on the dirt road, wrote letters to people I had neglected, baked several loaves of banana bread to freeze, and went to bed to sleep with what the constellation had shown me. That night, after celebrating my life with work, I went to sleep. As they had a hundred times before, the storytellers came to me.

I will always remember the stories they told and, as my ancestors gently gave this story to me, I now give it to you.

28

CARRYING TREAJURE

Once there was a young woman. Her eyes were the brown of a forest trail after an autumn rain, the color of the secret shaded parts of the bristle cone pinecone. Her eyes were full of joy in a way that would make the old men smile and the old women laugh. She was made with a heart that had a place for love as big and open as the meadow that sang through the new grass in the spring.

Some young men could hunt in a way that brought stories that kept children awake until their eyes burned. They would talk of their hearts pounding; tell of an arrow that had turned magic at the moment a buck bounded around a hill. They were young men who were loved by the children for the jerky they carried, that came with a tale about the secret moment that the deer had offered to be their treat.

One day, the young woman, with her open heart, felt one of the young men watching her. Watching her like a hunter who decides that this is a time that he will just look, just admire. Bending and digging roots, she felt him picking her out of the group of women she was with. As she laughed with them, she began to feel his heart beating and her heart beat with it. For a long time, he sat on the hill, under a tree. She bent over with her stick, searching for roots and, occasionally, like the doe, she would pop up her head and search under the tree to see that the young hunter was still there. After weeks of him watching her digging, he came to her father's house with an offer of elk meat. He asked if the young woman had enough room in her heart to love him. Everyone had been watching them and knew that her heart was made to love him, and more.

The two young people were beautiful to see. She fed children and old ones with her love; he fed them with his meat. Many campfires were filled with laughing as he told the stories of other men running while he stood before a bear asking him to fight. Children whispered to their Mothers, "Is that true?" as they chewed on bear meat and he told how he shot the bear for rudely walking away from his challenge. As his heart beat with the story, the young woman smiled as she listened to her heartbeat, and with it, she could feel his heart pounding. Like two drums by the fire, she could always hear them both.

Her heart had such room for the love that filled night and day with the song of the two drums. And the woman with the brown eyes loved him as he amazed the children and fed her family.

One day, the young woman was digging and she felt the sky spin. The wind sucked the spit from her mouth and her stomach was filled with a stone that she did not see enter her body. She fell to the ground and she listened, confused. She felt her heart beat so loudly that she could not hear the trees talking. She listened and she began to feel sweat on her lip as she heard her heart beat…and listened… and listened, but could not find the heart beat of her hunter.

Her body became weak and, as the sun went down, she found herself surrounded by women who cut her hair and sang to her. One very old woman came to her and said, "You have lost your young man. In your arms now, you have pain. As the snow comes, you will want to stop carrying the pain. You may want to put it into your heart because you think that will be an easy place to carry it but the heart is not made to carry pain. I can tell you that I have lost many men. You must learn to let your arms become strong and you will learn how to carry the pain. You cannot change your heart by asking it to carry this because you get tired." The old woman told her, "I can tell you this because my heart still has room for love". The old woman smiled at her and she quietly held the young woman who held the pain in her arms, rocking it like a baby. The old woman told her, " Pick up your pain like firewood. Tie it in bundles. I hope that you will have, in your lifetime a very small bundle. But know that if you are not lazy, you will be able to carry the bundles that you find on your path. That is the way that it is supposed to be".

Day by day the woman rocked the pain, and sang to it, and eventually she could carry the pain on her hip while she worked, and her heart still had a place for love.

Over the years, like the old woman, many men that she had in her heart died. Each time she remembered what the woman said, and she ached trying to find a way to carry the pain. Her heart stayed open and when the people saw her coming they could see this place of love.

One day a new warrior came to her; a new baby that had come from her body. This love grew as he played and looked at her in a way that made her heart excited, like first frost after the sun comes up, warm and cool at the same time. Her heart was filled with the love for that child. She watched and loved and smiled as she felt his little heartbeat with hers until, one day, she looked and felt the strength of his heart beat and knew that he was a man.

The day that she felt his heart stop beating, she could not get up. All of her bundles that she had learned to hold, fell and she could not organize them. This new pain could not be wrapped, her hips and back ached as she struggled to find where she could keep it. She felt room in her heart, and she would have tried to carry some of her pain bundles in there but she remembered the voice of the old woman as she tried to stand and gather her bundles.

She remembered the love of the old woman when the first bundle had come to her and she promised the woman that she would not to lose the room she had in her heart for love; but she found no way she could carry all the bundles.

The woman wailed as she walked and fell and tried to carry them all. Her knees bled and her arms were wrapped with the red of the buck brush scratches as she fought to get to the top of the mountain with all her bundles. It seemed as though it took her lifetimes to get to the top of the mountain. The spirit of the old woman, who had talked with her in her youth, walked with her to the top of the mountain. The spirit of the old woman sang to her as she wept. The old woman's spirit sang a song that told her that she was strong enough to carry the pain. The woman with all the bundles screamed as her muscles cramped while she climbed and tried to carry all the bundles. Falling, weeping, unable to be still and feel the horrible echo of her single heartbeat; the woman climbed, carried by the old woman's song, to the top of the mountain.

The woman could not carry all the bundles so she lay under the sky, her brown eyes dull and shining, like the damp earth over an otter tunnel on the bank of a river. She lay on the ground and tried to pull all her bundles together so that she could hold them all, so that she could find a way to rock them all, to sing to them, and keep her heart open for love. And the old woman stayed with her, and sang for her, and rocked her as she tried to find a way to hold all of her bundles at once. The woman would sleep as the old spirit sang and, when still she could not carry all her bundles, she just sat, not knowing what to do.

As the woman sat, the spirit of the old woman told her that she could do something. She should not just sit. So the woman began to weave. She gathered the grasses around her where she sat. Trying to keep all her pain bundles close, she gathered the twigs where she sat. She pulled the grass and felt the sweet juice in her dry mouth as she added each blade. And she began to weave. As she wove, the old woman sang to her. She ached with tired as she tried to weave and keep all her bundles next to her.

As the woman sat, a Woodpecker watched. He beat on a tree in the rhythm of the old woman's song and he watched the woman weeping, and weaving, and trying to find a way to organize her bundles.

The Woodpecker saw the love of the woman and he flew by to give her a gift. As the woman wove, she felt the bright red feather brush against her cheek. She carefully found a place to put the feather in the basket that she had started to weave. Woodpecker's cousins, the Turkey, the Red-Tail Hawk, the Raven, and the Blue Jay all heard about the woman's love and all of her pain bundles. They each, in their turn flew by to give her a gift. Even the river brothers: the Eagle, the Osprey, the White Egret and the Blue Heron, came from over the mountain and brought their feather gifts. And each gift found its way into the basket. The spirit of the old woman sang, the woman wove, and the spirit of the old woman fed her while she wove.

For many days, all the people mourned for the woman. They talked about how she had wandered off. They talked about how it was easy to see how she would not be able to carry so many bundles. They missed her and they missed her love.

One day, the woman looked and saw that her basket had gotten very large. She sat, and she looked, and quietly, and with great care, she began to put all of her bundles into the basket. She looked at the huge basket on her lap and she saw that there would even be room for more bundles. She wove a strap to go around her shoulders so that the basket could be carried, even as heavy as it was. The woman stood up and she put her basket, which was full of the bundles over her back. And she walked back down the hill to her family.

One little girl saw the woman first but the child felt caught in a dream as she saw more colors than the river has rocks glistening like feathers in the sun, as the woman came toward the village. The little girl ran and told the woman's family and all the people. They all came running to see the woman.

As they came toward her, they all stopped. There was the woman, walking toward them; her heart was open for love and on her back was a burden basket like none had ever seen. Red, blue, silver, orange, feathers of every color floated around the basket.

Everyone chattered like magpies about the beauty of the basket. The woman smiled as children touched the feathers, and old women looked at her and her basket.

The woman walked into the village with all her bundles, and her heart open, and none but she knew the weight of the basket.

Kaan kwasi kwaiyahkwa!
(The End of the Story: Literal Translation in Shoshone: The Rat's tail came off!)

GRANDMOTHER

Grandmother,
With you goes the child
Who wintered outside of Elko
And summered in the hills.

With you goes the woman
Who taught me of "Anzi"*
Not just any ants,
But the little black sweet ones.

With you go the bright artist's afghans
And a trail of rainbow quilts.
With you go the hands
Reminiscent of walnut shells,
As firm as a horse trainer's
Yet as gentle as a new
Black haired baby's.

Grandmother,
With you go the lavenders,
Gardens that loved you
And every sagebrush blossom that you noticed.
With you goes the woodstove,
The frying sage hen
And the pie drawer.
But, I thank you that
With me stays
Ne Kaku*

-Francesca Mason Boring

*Anzi: Shoshone for black ants
*_ne kaku_: Shoshone for maternal Grandmother

Printed in the United States
83842LV00004B/157-180/A